"You Don't Want Me to Kiss You, Do You."

There was a certainty in Kyle's words that made them a statement. Was it disappointment she was seeing in his otherwise shuttered expression?

Neither one of them had moved. Toni held his gaze steadily. This was her chance. He was handing her an opportunity she couldn't pass up. She could feel the tension in Kyle's body. She knew he was waiting. The next move had to be hers.

She caught her bottom lip between her teeth as she hesitantly curved her arms around his neck. Kyle's eyes widened slightly, but he didn't move.

"Yes," Toni whispered. "I do want you to kiss me."

Dear Reader:

Nora Roberts, Tracy Sinclair, Jeanne Stephens, Carole Halston, Linda Howard. Are these authors familiar to you? We hope so, because they are just a few of our most popular authors who publish with Silhouette Special Edition each and every month. And the Special Edition list is changing to include new writers with fresh stories. It has been said that discovering a new author is like making a new friend. So during these next few months, be sure to look for books by Sandi Shane, Dorothy Glenn and other authors who have just written their first and second Special Editions, stories we hope you enjoy.

Choosing which Special Editions to publish each month is a pleasurable task, but not an easy one. We look for stories that are sophisticated, sensuous, touching, and great love stories, as well. These are the elements that make Silhouette Special Editions more romantic...and unique.

So we hope you'll find this Silhouette Special Edition just that—*Special*—and that the story finds a special place in your heart.

The Editors at Silhouette

SERL-7/85

CHRISTINE FLYNN
Remember the Dreams

Silhouette Special Edition

Published by Silhouette Books New York

America's Publisher of Contemporary Romance

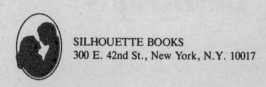

SILHOUETTE BOOKS
300 E. 42nd St., New York, N.Y. 10017

Copyright © 1985 by Christine Flynn

Distributed by Pocket Books

ISBN: 0-373-09254-7

First Silhouette books printing August, 1985

10 9 8 7 6 5 4 3 2 1

America's Publisher of Contemporary Romance

Printed in the U.S.A.
BC91

CRISTINE FLYNN
admits to two obsessions, reading and writing, and three "serious" preoccupations, gourmet cooking, her family (she has a daughter and a husband she unabashedly describes as the sexiest best friend a girl could ever have) and travel. She has tried everything from racing cars to modeling and spent ten years in the legal field before settling into what she loves best—turning her daydreams into romance novels.

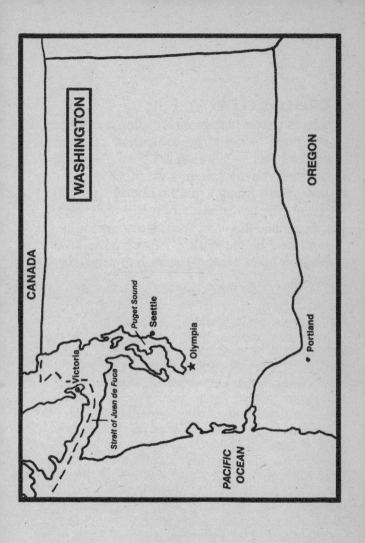

Chapter One

"Why don't you live with me, Toni?"

Antoinette Collins leveled her vivid blue eyes at Kyle Donovan and lowered her glass of wine. If Kyle had suggested such a thing five years ago—which he never would have—it would have been the fulfillment of her wildest fantasies. Though he'd never known, she'd been in love with him then.

Now Toni met his cool gray eyes easily, and a quiet pride filled her at what she had become. She was twenty-seven now. No longer the wide-eyed young woman he had once known. Her maturity was evident in the confident tilt of her head, the unconscious grace of her movements.

The light filtering through the University Club's arched windows created a platinum halo around the neat coil of her waist-length, flaxen hair and lent an alabaster sheen to her smooth complexion. She looked like an angel, but beneath her tailored suit jacket beat the heart of a dedicated and capable stockbroker. Only her inner softness, which she seldom allowed anyone to see, kept her from being a true Kyle Donovan creation.

A teasing light crept into her eyes as she considered what Kyle had just offered. "Are you serious?"

"Sure," he replied blithely, then took another sip of his wine. "Like I said, I'm out of town most of the time, so you'd practically have free run of the place. And since your company won't be picking up your hotel tab after tomorrow, it would give you more time to find a place of your own. You said yourself that you haven't had time to look since you were transferred back here." That sexy grin she remembered so well creased his darkly attractive features. "How about it?"

Toni leaned back in her chair, contemplating the man she hadn't seen in five years. His fascinating gray eyes still reflected the determination that had made him a name partner in the nationally known brokerage house she used to work for. The evidence of his success was apparent in the abundance of silver woven through his casually styled black hair and the more prominent depth of the lines bracketing his firm and sensual mouth. He always used to be in such a hurry, his pace leaving lesser men—or women—floundering in his wake. He played hard, and worked harder. But his compulsion seemed to have given way to a more comfortable, less aggressive manner. Though she didn't doubt that that aggression still lurked beneath the surface, he seemed more relaxed now. The way he carried his lean, athletic frame spoke of calm self-assurance, and his casualness made his arresting features even more compelling.

Toni immediately dismissed her last thought, along with the odd quickening of her pulse. It was only fatigue—or maybe the second glass of wine—that was causing her to wonder what that beautiful mouth would feel like against hers. Kyle had never kissed her. He'd never even come close. They were nothing more than friends, and she knew that the only reason he had called her—after reading in the local business paper that she was now managing a competitor's office—was because of the friendship they had once shared.

Before she'd left Seattle to work for another firm in New York, Kyle had been her boss, her mentor, her confidant. The ease with which they had met again proved that the intervening years had done little to change that unique relationship. It seemed like only yesterday that they had sat at this same table either heatedly debating the merits of investing in futures, or discussing Kyle's rather hectic love life. Kyle had always played Russian Roulette with his lovers—but he hadn't known how his innocent comments about those women had hurt Toni.

She'd adored him. But she had hidden her emotions well.

Kyle's forehead had pleated in a questioning frown, and Toni realized that she'd been quiet for too long. Jerking herself from her reverie, she returned to the matter he had brought up only moments ago.

"Don't you think that my presence might cramp your style?" she prodded, seriously entertaining his offer. What he was proposing sounded perfect, and very practical. Toni was always practical.

The frown faded. "I'll have you know that I'm considerably more circumspect now than I was in my youth." The solemnity of his words was ruined with his devilish grin.

"Your youth! You were thirty years old!"

"So I was a late bloomer," he shrugged.

"If you were a late bloomer," she returned dryly, "then I was . . ."

Still struggling for an analogy, she saw Kyle lean forward. The glint of a gold cufflink edged from the sleeve of his impeccable gray jacket as he crossed his arms on the small cocktail table.

"A snow princess?" he offered, a conspiratorial gleam in his eyes.

She'd stepped right into that one. Kyle had always found it quite amusing, if not incredible, that then, at twenty-two, Toni had yet to sacrifice her virtue.

"That's not what I was going to say. And," she supplied succinctly, "I think I'm a little old for that title."

She was admitting to nothing, and he could draw his own conclusions from her statement. It seemed important that he think of her as something other than the "snow princess." He probably wouldn't believe it if he knew the truth anyway. Toni was convinced that she was the only twenty-seven-year-old virgin left on the face of the earth.

A soft smile curved her lips. So little had changed between them. She could still say exactly what she wanted to say—she'd never wanted to tell him how she'd once felt—and apparently Kyle also felt that same freedom. It was one of the things she had valued so highly about their friendship.

The amusement slipped from his eyes as he settled back. His intent gray gaze moved slowly from the smooth part of her hair, over the sultry sweep of her dark lashes, then stopped briefly on the generous curve of her mouth. His eyes seemed to linger there before settling on the provocative expanse of skin revealed above the third button of her blouse.

The appraisal was one she had been subjected to many times before, but never by Kyle. And never had it seemed so invasive, so thorough.

The large room suddenly made her feel almost claustrophobic.

When he glanced back up at her questioning eyes, none of the male appreciation she'd just seen was even remotely evident.

Had she just imagined it?

"Too bad," he decreed with mock gravity. "The last of an endangered species finally bit the dust. I presume that the man in question offered to do the honorable thing?"

There really was no "man in question." The only relationship of any substance she'd had, had been with a man who was so much like Kyle it was positively uncanny. The "affair" hadn't taken the usual course, but Kyle didn't need to know that.

"No," she said, forcing the lightness from her voice. She didn't want to change the conclusion he'd obviously drawn.

Kyle regarded her steadily, his expression hardening as he saw the smile fading from her eyes.

He didn't know that she was trying to keep from laughing.

"Did he hurt you, princess?"

A little surprised at the anger tightening his jaw and the contradicting softness of his question, Toni hastily assured him that "he" hadn't. "No real damage done," she returned. At least that remark was totally honest. "It was a classic case of inexperienced, naive young woman meets dashing and worldly male whose only desire is to add her to his trophy collection. You," she teased with an accusing arch of her eyebrow. ". . . should certainly recognize the scenario." She was doing nothing to correct his assumption.

"Ouch!" Kyle clutched his heart as if he'd been mortally wounded, then glanced at her narrowly. "Maybe it wouldn't be such a good idea having you around after all. You'd stop at nothing to remind me of my tainted past."

Remembering how much fun it used to be to bait him, she shot him a look of feigned disapproval. "If you hadn't told me about all of your conquests . . ." She let the sentence trail off meaningfully.

"I didn't *tell* you about them," he defended. "I just asked you what to *do* about them."

"Same difference," she returned airily. "And I

never did understand why you wanted my advice. You were the one with all the experience."

Cupping the bowl of his glass in his large hands, Kyle glanced down at it. He seemed to be studying the pale golden wine. "Maybe it was because you were always so level-headed when it came to relationships."

Toni refused to find any deeper meaning in his words. He wasn't talking about their relationship and she knew it. Instead, she opted to pick up on the subject he'd just reopened. "Staying with you might pose a few problems, you know. It seemed like we always used to wind up in an argument about something and . . ."

"But they were friendly arguments," he interrupted, his eyes dancing over her delicate features. "I just played devil's advocate to your overly simplistic rationale about everything from how to cure the national debt to life in general."

"Overly simplistic!" Toni's animated expression relaxed in a barely suppressed smile. It was pointless to defend ideals that had long since been proven wrong. But for the sake of the argument, and to prove her point, she added, "At least I wasn't a cynic! And I wasn't the one who could take a straightforward transaction and complicate it to the point—"

The expression on Kyle's face stopped her abruptly. He was watching her with the mildly amused grin that used to drive her crazy. Like he was indulging a precocious child.

"I guess we've both changed a little," he said mildly. "You know, I'd always wondered what happened to my snow princess, but I didn't realize how much I'd missed you until I saw you again. I'll try to make a point of being home for a few days next week so I can find out what you've been up to all these years."

My snow princess? Why did his use of the possessive cause her heart to take on such a chaotic beat? He'd meant nothing by it, she was sure of that. He was just the same old Kyle. Well, not *exactly* the same. But he wasn't treating her any differently from the way he always had.

"I'm in direct competition with your company." Mentioning a possible point of contention seemed safer than dwelling on something that didn't exist.

"So we don't discuss our accounts." His shoulders lifted in a dismissive shrug, and he scrawled his signature across the bill the waitress had unobtrusively presented. "That still leaves us with plenty to talk about. After you fill me in on your life, you can help me straighten out a little situation I've found myself involved in . . . and then there's always politics, religion and . . ."—he gave her a playful leer—"sex."

If he was expecting her to blush like she would have when he used to tease her, he'd have a very long wait. Working on Wall Street had provided a very sophisticated education, and Toni had learned most of those lessons quite well. Instead of lowered lashes, Toni was blessed with a boldly level glance and an indulgent sigh.

The "little situation" he'd just mentioned quite probably had something to do with a woman. Toni was actually thankful that he was involved with someone, but she couldn't figure out why. What difference did it make?

"You and I both know that those are three subjects that virtually guarantee an argument, Mr. Donovan."

If he was trying to look innocent, he was failing miserably. "Are you saying that we're incompatible?"

The curve of her mouth drew upward, a glimmer of pure pleasure lighting the tiny flecks of green in her blue eyes. "Undoubtedly."

"Guess it's a good thing I won't be around much then." Pushing his chair back, he drew his six-foot-two-inch frame up to its imposing height. Even at five-foot-seven, Toni had always felt dwarfed by him. "Let's go get you checked out of the hotel."

"Now?" She hadn't actually said she'd accept his offer, though she guessed her acceptance had been implied.

"Why not? Living in a hotel for three weeks is bound to be getting to you. And with the schedule you've been keeping, you need to be someplace where you can relax." He pulled her chair out and, sliding his hand beneath her elbow, drew her to her feet. "I've got a hot tub and a sauna that you can use without having to share it with anyone else, and when you get home from work you can kick your feet up on the deck and listen to nothing but the wind in the trees. I make a point of doing it just as often as I can."

He was still her mentor. Only the lesson he was imparting now was quite different from the one she'd been tutored in so long ago. She'd become everything he'd taught her to be. Hard-working and totally dedicated. And in that scheme there was no room for such unnecessary things as relaxation. Could he see the toll that that type of existence was taking on her? Had he recognized it in himself? Maybe that was why she'd noted so many subtle differences in him.

But it didn't begin to explain why he was looking at her like this.

Standing in front of him, her head tilted back slightly and her blue eyes locked on his fathomless gray ones, Toni suddenly felt like she was sinking through the floor. The walls of the room seemed to be receding and even the quiet conversations taking place at the other tables had faded away.

Kyle's face was devoid of expression, and her own mirrored that strange intensity. An intangible electricity filled the very air surrounding them. Toni was vaguely aware of his deep, indrawn breath and the almost imperceptible tightening of his hand on her elbow. She had the craziest urge to reach up and touch the hard line of his jaw, to run her finger over those sensual lips. With a deliberate effort, she curled her hand at her side.

In the next instant whatever it was that she'd seen in his eyes was gone, replaced with his easy smile. It was as if whatever it was that had happened, hadn't happened at all.

"Come on, kid." His use of the subordinate term effectively erased the last traces of the rather disconcerting moment. "I've got a flight to catch in three hours." He nudged her across the room. "That's just enough time to get you settled in and me packed and to the airport."

Toni had learned that the matter-of-fact approach always netted the best results in any given situation. Practically speaking, there was no reason why she shouldn't stay with Kyle. They were friends—platonic friends, she firmly reminded herself. Anything else she might be feeling was just a nostalgic memory of something she'd felt five years ago.

Pulling her rented Pontiac up behind Kyle's black Porsche, Toni gaped at the sprawling redwood and glass structure nestled in a forest of fir trees. The road winding up the hill ended there, and there wasn't another house in sight. If Kyle had wanted a place where he could get away from everything, this was definitely it.

"I'll put your suitcases in the last room on the left," Kyle said, motioning her through the double doors and nodding toward a wide hallway off the entry. "Take a look around while I pack."

Descending the steps leading into the sunken living room, Toni's eyebrows arched approvingly. An enormous window overlooking Puget Sound comprised the far wall of the spacious, high-ceilinged room—a room her entire apartment back in New York would have fit inside quite easily. The pearl gray drapes, which matched the thick carpeting, were drawn back, exposing a redwood deck that ran the length of the house. Dusk was giving way to darkness, and over the tops of the trees, she could see the city lights glimmering off in the distance.

A curving leather sofa, in a deep gray that Toni thought matched the color of Kyle's eyes, occupied the center of the room. Moving toward it, she dropped her purse on one of the glass tables between it and a navy blue chair. Kyle had said to take a look around, and that was exactly what she was going to do.

Everything from the glassed-in pool downstairs to the panoramic views available from nearly every room in the house lent to the air of quiet luxury and relaxation. But as she returned to the main level, an uncomfortable thought accompanied her. She'd seen a couple of guest rooms downstairs. So where had Kyle put her things? Was the "last room on the left" *his* room?

"Toni?" Kyle's voice was muffled by the maze of walls separating them.

Telling herself that she was being ridiculous for even entertaining such an idea, she followed the sound of that deep, resonant voice. She moved down the wide hallway, peeking into rooms as she went, and stopped at the end of the hall.

Her luggage was sitting inside a large, comfortable room to her left. Kyle was standing in the one to her right.

She didn't realize that she'd been holding her breath until she let it out. At the same time, she rubbed her clammy palms down the sides of her skirt. Of course Kyle had given her her own room. What had ever made her think otherwise?

Turning, she leaned against the doorjamb to watch Kyle.

He'd taken off his jacket, and his white shirt had been pulled free of his slacks. Judging from the way its tails hung loosely around his lean hips, the front of it was unbuttoned.

"Nice place," she observed, her eyes on the suitcase he'd laid on his bed—a large circular bed that seemed to dominate the room. "Were you dating an interior decorator?"

"No," he returned, dropping several pairs of jockey shorts into the suitcase. "I *hired* one. Is your room ok?"

Why did the sight of that bed make her so uncomfortable? Deciding that it was less unnerving to stare at the wrinkles in his shirttail, she replied, "It's perfect. How long will you be gone?" She didn't want to talk about bedrooms.

"Four days." A stack of neatly folded shirts joined the jockey shorts. "I'm giving a training seminar in Chicago. Come on in."

He turned then, moving toward the sliding glass mirrors of his closet.

Toni's mouth went dry.

His shirt *was* unbuttoned. Her blue eyes riveted to the crisp black hair covering the hard contours of his broad chest. The only direction she could seem to make them move in was down, and she followed that tapering line over his flat stomach to where the swirls disappeared beneath the waistband of his slacks.

Toni had only seen Kyle in his expensively tailored suits, or, at the very least, in an open-collared sport shirt and slacks. But even her vivid imagination hadn't done justice to his physical perfection.

Good heavens, Toni, she chided herself. He's just your average Greek god, so stop staring at him like this.

Admonishment was one thing. Practicing what she was preaching to herself was another matter entirely.

There was something terribly intimate about watching him like this—with him apparently quite comfortable with her presence—and a warm tingling seemed to center in the pit of her stomach.

Kyle reached into the closet, then glanced back over his shoulder. "Come on in," he repeated, indicating a wide doorway with a nod of his dark head. "The hot tub's in there. I want to show you how to turn it on before I go."

She couldn't move. Her hands felt clammy again, and her legs didn't want to cooperate with the command her apparently addled brain was giving them.

Seeing her apprehensive expression, Kyle walked toward her. Obviously he'd mistaken the reason for her reticence. "It's not that complicated," he chuckled, taking her hand and leading her across the springy carpet. "It's just a switch and a couple of buttons."

His hand felt so warm, so strong, and Toni tried her best to ignore the staccato shocks racing up her arm. She caught a whiff of his faintly spicy aftershave mingling with the heat of his body, the scent adding a frightening awareness to her already muddled senses.

It had to be fatigue. That was the only plausible explanation for why she should be reacting like this. Days that began at 5:00 A.M. when the exchange opened on the East Coast and didn't end until 10:00 at night after a meeting with a prospective investor were bound to catch up with her sooner or later. Rest. That's what she needed. Just a couple of days' rest.

"I think I can handle that," she smiled, feeling better now that she had analyzed her problem. "But I don't think I'll be using it."

"Why not?"

"Because my bathing suit's in storage with everything else."

He tossed her a sideways grin, his eyes traveling quickly down the length of her slender frame. "You don't need one."

Her response was little more than a faint rush of breath. There was no sense arguing the point unless it became necessary.

Averting her eyes to the placid pool of water at her feet, she almost jumped out of her skin when it suddenly sprang to life.

"This switch turns on the jets. . . ."

Toni barely heard what Kyle was saying. The image that had just formed in her mind refused to vanish. She could see him relaxing in that tub, the water swirling around that magnificent chest, his arm draped around her naked shoulders. She could almost feel his lean hardness pressing against her thighs, her breasts . . .

"And I try to keep it at around a hundred and one or so."

"Ah . . . I'm sorry," she mumbled, giving her head a visible shake to dispel the unwanted image. Not fatigue. It had to be total exhaustion for her mind to be working like this. "I guess I wasn't listening."

Kyle watched her curiously as he explained

again, his eyes following the motion of her hand.
She was running the pearl she wore back and
forth along its fine gold chain at the base of her
throat. It was a nervous habit, and an unconscious one.

A soft light crept into his eyes. Placing one
hand on her shoulder, he tipped her chin up with
his other. His touch, coming so closely on the
heels of her erratic—and erotic—thoughts, made
her legs feel about as stable as gelatin.

"You look beat, princess," he said quietly, his
gaze sweeping her pale features. His hand left
her shoulder to push back a whisp of golden hair
that had loosened itself from its coil.

Though his fingers barely brushed her cheek,
the skin there tingled with a lingering warmth.

"Why don't you go see what you can find in the
fridge for dinner while I finish packing? I've got
to leave in about twenty minutes."

She was sure that what she was seeing in
those beautiful slate-gray eyes was only the concern one friend might feel for another. If there
was any desire there, it was only the desire that
she get out of his way so he wouldn't miss his
plane.

"Do you want me to fix you something?" she
asked as his hands slipped to his sides.

Kyle shook his head and turned into his bedroom. "I'll get something later. If you can't find
what you want in the kitchen, leave a note for
Madeline next to the phone in there. She'll pick
up anything you want from the store."

"Who's Madeline?" All sorts of pictures were
forming in Toni's mind.

"My housekeeper. She does everything but

tuck me into bed at night. She'd probably even do that if I asked her to."

Toni didn't doubt that for a minute. She couldn't imagine any woman refusing Kyle Donovan anything.

She had just dropped her apple core into the trash compactor when she heard Kyle's footsteps crossing the parquet-tiled floor.

"Is that all you ate?"

"I wasn't that hungry," she replied, turning to lean against the counter. She'd left her suit jacket in her bedroom, along with her shoes. Without the benefit of two-and-a-half-inch heels it seemed that she had to look a long way up to see his face.

"You're too thin," he observed flatly, positioning himself against the counter next to her. "I thought you looked like you'd filled out a little when I first saw you, but now I actually think you're skinnier."

A disconcerted frown creased her forehead as she glanced down at the cream silk blouse tucked into her straight skirt. Skinnier? She'd gained five pounds!

"Let's see what else we can find you to eat."

"I'm really not hungry." Her words fell on deaf ears as he started to open the cupboard. "I had a big lunch."

Kyle looked down at her, one hand resting on the cupboard door. "I can only imagine what constitutes 'big' for you." A droll smile tugged at the corners of his mouth, deepening those delicious little laugh lines. "You probably had a couple of soda crackers and a few pieces of dry lettuce. Why are you women always on a diet?"

The only "diet" Toni had ever been on was to *gain* weight. "I'm not on one," she mumbled, taking a step back. It never used to bother her to stand next to him. Why did it now? "And I had a salad for lunch . . . with crab in it."

"Appropriate," he muttered, baiting her just as he used to. "But you need more protein. It's good for your nerves."

Her nerves could certainly use any help they could get. They'd definitely been acting a little haywire for the past few hours.

Kyle's remark about her thinness wasn't helping much either. And one of her insecurities was beginning to show.

Toni had always been self-conscious about her body. Where most women had curves, she had little dips and dents. Lanky and svelte had been her mother's charitable way of describing tall and skinny. Toni had been the only girl in her high school graduating class who had still been wearing a training bra.

Instead of withdrawing into herself, she had learned to turn a slightly aggressive cheek. Placing both hands on her "skinny" hips, she smugly met his intoxicating smile. "You don't have to play brother-protector anymore, Kyle. I think I can manage my own care and feeding." She watched his thick dark brows quirk upward over his laughing eyes. "You may not have noticed, but I'm a big girl now."

There was nothing at all brotherly about the way his darkening gaze raked over her. Still leaning with his hand on the cupboard and his tie draped loosely over his fresh white shirt, he looked every inch the male predator. Cool, calculating and very, very dangerous.

"Woman," he corrected smoothly. "And I noticed."

His visual assessment would have shaken her to her toes had she not already determined the cause of her strange reactions to him. Exhaustion. Pure and simple.

"But I've also noticed a few other things, *Ms.* Collins. You and I are going to have a long talk when I get back. So be sure and reserve Friday night for me."

"Which lecture am I going to get this time?" Her tone was teasing, her expression animated. "You can save your breath if you're planning on giving me the one about my 'overly simplistic' views, because, unfortunately, most of your theories have been proven right."

Toni was sure that she only imagined the slight hardening in his eyes. "Maybe I've developed a few new ones," he said.

"And I'm to be blessed with your infinite insight and wisdom?"

"Of course." He abandoned the cabinet and pulled open the freezer. "I always used to share my vast and formidable experience with you, so why should it be any different now?" He dropped a gallon of ice cream on the counter. "That's what friends are for, you know?" He placed a bowl and spoon next to the carton. "Eat this."

"Too many calories," she returned blandly, knowing that the second he was gone, she'd help herself to a healthy scoop.

"I thought you said you weren't on a diet?"

"I'm not." She grinned at him then, enjoying the familiar ease of their exchange. "I'm only . . ."

"Being obstinate," he concluded for her. "You always did like to see how far you could push me."

Her expression was one of angelic innocence, except for the mischievous twinkle in her eyes. "I did?"

"You know you did." Moving past her, he headed out of the kitchen. "But I don't think you ever had any idea of how far you'd gone."

"What's that supposed to mean?" Her question was directed at his retreating back.

Following him through the dining room, she stopped when they reached the entry. Kyle picked up his jacket from the table by the front door and, tossing it over his arm, bent to retrieve the flight bag sitting on the floor.

"There's an extra house key on your dresser," he said, completely ignoring her question. "I'll be at the Chicago Hilton if you need to reach me for anything."

Seconds later, he was gone.

Toni stood staring blankly at the carved oak doors, his strangely spoken words echoing in her ears. *But I don't think you ever had any idea of how far you'd gone.*

Years ago she would have spent hours dwelling on his mysterious comment. But now, she gave it no further thought. She'd spent enough time trying to figure him out five years ago to know that she'd never understand what motivated him.

He'd been married once. But the circumstances surrounding his divorce were known only to Kyle and his never-mentioned ex-wife. He'd once told Toni that marriage demanded something he could never give, and the cold finality in his voice had abruptly ended any further discussion on the subject.

She had always wondered if that was why he seemed to hold a part of himself back—the part that made him unattainable by the women in his life.

Toni did understand one thing about him though. Kyle loved a challenge. Any challenge. Whether it was a way to play the stock market, beating an opponent at tennis, or a woman. Once he had won, he immediately became bored with his trophy and moved on to something else. It was almost as if he were trying to prove something to himself—that he could have whatever he wanted.

Toni had never known him to lose.

It hadn't been until she'd been away from Kyle for over a year that she'd realized how wrong he would have been for her—even if he had been interested. Whatever it was that drove him, nurtured that streak of ruthlessness, also made him scoff at the very things she wanted most.

Toni was still very much a romantic, though a practiced veneer of sophistication covered it. A closet romantic since she had learned how people laugh at such idealistic attitudes. But she still harbored the dream that someday she would fall in love with someone, marry and bear his children. The career that came first now would willingly be given second place. Right now though, that career was all she had,

Undoubtedly Kyle would still laugh at her old-fashioned ideas. People can't change their basic beliefs any more easily than a leopard can change its spots. Kyle seemed to have softened a little, but he couldn't possibly have changed that much. Not that it mattered. Despite their differences, he was and always would be her friend. A very special friend.

Toni was certain that, this time, she was in no danger of falling in love with him. She didn't bother to wonder why it was so necessary to reassure herself of that.

Chapter Two

The last thing Toni expected when she returned to Kyle's house Friday night, was to see him sitting on the front steps. An irritated scowl creased his darkly attractive features, and as he glanced up at her he looked anything but pleased.

"Forget your key?" she asked, her heels tapping on the flagstone walkway as she approached. Holding her key out to him, she slowly lowered her hand. One of the double doors behind him was slightly ajar.

Her eyebrows lowered sharply as she glanced back to where he was sitting. Judging from the half-empty wineglass he was holding and the casual denims and pullover he was wearing, it was obvious that he'd been home for a while. Whatever it was that was causing him to look so disgruntled wasn't that he'd locked himself out.

"No, I didn't forget my key," he replied dryly. Averting his glance from her puzzled expression, he pulled himself to his feet. When he looked back down at her there was the faintest trace of a smile in his narrowed eyes. "I was beginning to think that you'd forgotten something though. I asked you to keep tonight open for me. Remember?"

Oh, she remembered! But she had managed to convince herself that it was the pile of work on her desk—and not because she was a little nervous about seeing Kyle again—that had kept her at the office past seven o'clock.

It was apparent that he was trying to shake his dark mood, but Toni could still sense his tension. The way the hard line of his jaw was working was a dead giveaway.

Toni knew that she'd be giving herself far too much credit to think that he was upset because she was late. She knew better. Never had she known Kyle to get upset about anything except what mattered to him. And all that really mattered to Kyle Donovan was work.

Smiling up at him, a flicker of understanding in her bright blue eyes, she shook her neatly coiffed head. "I can still read you like a book, Donovan." He glared down at her and her smile broadened. "I'm sure that the prospect of being stood up by your roommate isn't the reason you were sitting here looking like you were ready to kill. Do you want to tell me what went wrong in Chicago out here? Or"—glancing down at her tailored black suit, she tugged at the bow on her white blouse—"can I get comfortable first?"

His expression was only slightly less forbidding when he took her briefcase and motioned her inside. "Get comfortable," he said, stepping back to let her pass. "Then you can help me finish getting dinner ready."

Toni gave him a curt little nod and headed toward her room. The edge in his voice made her a little uneasy. Maybe he *was* irritated with her.

Immediately dismissing that idea, she quickly changed into a pair of slacks and a black oxford shirt. She'd never known Kyle to be on time for anything, unless it involved business, so he couldn't possibly be angry with her for being a couple of hours late. It wasn't that she was *late* anyway. He hadn't even told her what time he'd be home.

"Ok," she began the second she entered the kitchen. "What happened in Chicago?"

Expecting to hear some disaster that had befallen his seminar, she crossed her arms and tilted her head thoughtfully. The skylights in the kitchen ceiling were dark now, but the bright overhead lights made her smoothly coiled hair look almost white.

"What makes you think something happened there?" Turning, he handed her a glass of wine.

His guileless expression held absolutely no trace of a frown, and he regarded her steadily. If she hadn't seen it herself, she wouldn't have believed that the man grinning at her now was the same one she'd met on the porch only minutes ago.

Genuinely perplexed by his sudden change, she reached for the goblet and studied him warily. "I guess I just thought that something must have happened at the seminar for you to be acting so . . ."

"So . . . what?" he prodded when she didn't continue.

Lifting her slender shoulders in a shrug, she turned away. "Never mind," she muttered, raising the glass to her lips. He obviously didn't want to discuss whatever it was, and she wasn't about to pry. Maybe it had something to do with that "little situation" he'd mentioned the other night. If that was the case, she was pretty sure she'd hear about it sooner or later.

Looking around the spacious kitchen, cryptically noting the array of electrical gadgets occupying the beige tiled counters—a food processor, blender, coffeepot, knife sharpener, toaster—she glanced back toward him. "Plug me in and tell me what you want me to do."

Having seen the path her inspection had taken, he mumbled, "Cute," and nodded toward the salad sitting in a wooden bowl next to the sink. "Toss it," he instructed as he liberally seasoned two thick steaks.

Her task took all of fifteen seconds. Taking another sip of wine, she leaned against the counter to watch him. She was careful to note only how easily he moved about the kitchen, and pointedly ignored the way his flat knit sweater molded the muscular contours of his broad back. Each movement caused those muscles to flex and smooth, and she refused to think about how solid they must feel. Her throat felt a little dry, but she told herself that it had nothing to do with the fact that her eyes were now glued to the soft fabric clinging to his lean hips, or that he had just turned around and she was staring at his zipper.

Mercifully, he didn't notice the path her eyes had taken this time.

"So," he said, shoving the steaks under the broiler. "What did you do all week?"

Her throat didn't feel dry. It was positively parched. A gulp of wine was in order. "Well," she began, with a hasty cough. "You know that the market was up, so things have . . ."

"Not at the office," he interrupted, taking the goblet she was clutching a little too tightly and handing her two pottery plates. "Put these on the table. I meant other than that. I can imagine what your days are like."

She sat the plates on the oak and glass table on the far side of the kitchen. "Unfortunately, the nights are about the same." Returning to the silverware drawer, she handed him the knives and forks. "Put these on the table," she smiled sweetly, handing him the utensils. "But I did go to a show Wednesday night."

She started to tell him what movie she'd seen, but he cut in too quickly.

"Who with?"

"One of our investors."

His thick eyebrows arched slightly. "I've never taken a client to a show to get business before, but whatever tactic works . . ." His sentence was completed with an absent shrug.

"It wasn't business."

Kyle seemed to be taking more time than was

necessary positioning the silverware around the plates. "Someone you've been seeing much of?"

"That was the first time I went out with him," she returned, realizing how silly the fears that had plagued her all afternoon had been. There was no reason to be nervous with Kyle. She actually felt more comfortable with him now than she had five years ago. "But he's taking me to dinner tomorrow night," she added, watching Kyle reposition the forks.

The fork hit the floor and Kyle returned to get another.

"Sounds like you're interested in the guy." Kyle's tone was bland, but he wasn't looking at her. And the muscle in his jaw looked like it was going to start twitching again. "Think it could be anything serious?"

Hardly, she thought to herself. Dr. Greg Nichols was certainly nice enough, but he was more interested in free investment advice than anything else. She had thought his good-night kiss awfully . . . clinical. "After only one movie . . ." She glanced over at the oven. There was a fair amount of smoke curling over the door. ". . . It's way too soon to tell. I think your steaks are burning."

Kyle reached the oven in four long strides. The sound of its door crashing down muffled his terse "Damn!"

"I like mine rare," she taunted, careful to keep the smile from her face.

Casting her a quelling glare, he flipped the meat over with his fingers. The way he jerked his hand back after turning each steak was a pretty good indication of how hot they were. "You'll take it the way you get it," he grumbled.

Toni wasn't all that convinced that something hadn't gone wrong in Chicago, or that his "little situation" wasn't getting to be something more than he could handle. That had to be the reason he still seemed so irritable. Though she felt some sympathy for him—quite a bit actually—there was something about seeing Kyle in less than total control that was a little amusing. It made him seem so much more human, and less the idol he had once been.

Her facial muscles were flinching with a smile that didn't want to be suppressed. Putting her hand to her forehead, she looked down at the floor and tried to keep the laughter from her voice. "You know, Kyle, if you'd use a fork . . ."

"I wouldn't get burned." He completed the sentence sharply. He barely glanced at her as he pushed the pan back under the broiler. "Just because a person knows how to prevent something doesn't necessarily mean that he has the good sense to do it."

"My," she teased, ignoring the urge to push back the lock of hair that had fallen over his forehead, "that's an awfully profound statement for something as inconsequential as how to turn a steak."

It occurred to her then, as she watched the strong cords in his neck tense in agitation, that maybe he was talking about something else entirely.

"There's nothing particularly profound about stating the obvious." He didn't sound nearly as

curt as he had a moment before, and the tiny
lines etched around his eyes deepened with his
smile. "And it's also obvious that we can't cook
and talk at the same time. Why don't you put the
wine on the table and I'll bring these in a
minute."

Their conversation resumed as soon as dinner
was on their plates in relative safety.

"What kept you so late tonight?" Kyle asked,
absently reaching for the pepper.

It wouldn't do to say "nerves," so she just
mumbled, "Work," and took another bite of her
salad.

"Aren't things slacking up yet?"

"You said you didn't want to hear about it,"
she reminded him mockingly.

"Maybe I changed my mind."

"Well," she drawled, returning his grin, "if
that's the case . . ."

It took no further prodding for Toni to begin an
animated replay of everything that had happened during the week. The office had been in
near chaos when she'd taken over, but things
were finally taking shape. Though she'd had a
few problems with one of the account managers
who was refusing to pull his weight, matters
were now moving quite smoothly. She loved her
work and the pleasure she took in it was quite
evident.

More than that was apparent to Kyle though.

Kyle never approached a situation without
weighing all the possible consequences. At least
he hadn't until now. This morning he'd tempo-
rarily abandoned that philosophy.

Without allowing himself to question his reasons, he'd cut out on his last meeting and caught the earliest flight he could get back to Seattle. All he knew was that he wanted to see Toni, and when she hadn't shown up until almost eight o'clock, he'd been furious. Not with her. With himself. Toni had always represented the type of woman he never got involved with, but his compulsion to see her, to be with her, had obscured all rationality.

Sitting on the front steps for over two hours had helped restore the logic that had eluded him earlier. They were just friends. Nothing more. And he'd make darn sure things stayed that way.

Thank God she'd thought that he was upset over the seminar. If she'd had any idea of the crazy thoughts that had been tormenting him all week, she'd probably tip that proud little chin up and call him a pervert. It was obvious enough that she still thought of him as something of an older brother.

For the life of him he wished he could feel that same nonthreatening attachment to her. But the woman sitting across from him now seemed so different from the one he'd remembered. She still teased him like she used to, but all resemblance to that malleable young woman stopped there.

He'd never really noticed her voice before, how sultry it sounded. Enjoying the sound of it, enjoying watching her, he didn't even realize how intense his gaze had become.

He could have been eating filet mignon or sautéed cardboard for all the attention he was paying to his food. He was too busy savoring the grace of her hands as they punctuated a thought, the tilt of her head when she appeared thoughtful, the way her captivating blue eyes narrowed when she homed in on some obscure nuance of a transaction. Her eyes weren't really blue at all. They were aquamarine. Had he ever really noticed the jewellike flecks of green in them before?

His eyes moved slowly over her face and up to the silken coil of her hair. He tried to remember how she used to wear it, but couldn't. All he recalled was that it had been short. Collar length maybe? Now he wondered if those long tresses, caught up so chastely in that thick roll, were as soft as they looked. What would she do if he asked her to take it down?

He smiled to himself, imagining her reaction to such a request, and tried to concentrate on what she was saying.

But all Kyle could think about was that Antoinette Collins had turned into one very intelligent, incredibly sexy woman.

He'd never even met the guy she was going out with tomorrow night, but he was dead certain that he wasn't going to like him.

". . . and I think you would have done the same thing," Toni concluded, tossing her napkin onto her empty plate.

"I'm sure I would have," Kyle said, not even knowing what he was agreeing with. God, but she's got a beautiful mouth, he thought, knowing that if he didn't stop staring at it, he'd only succeed in resurrecting everything he was trying so hard not to think about. But the thought of those soft lips moving beneath his, caressing him the way he wanted to caress her, was causing problems with more than his concentration. "Let's go for a swim."

He'd found swimming a very effective way to cool off.

Toni's dark lashes narrowed. "But we just ate."

Kyle's napkin fell over his half-eaten dinner. "You won't sink."

"That's not what I meant," she returned, eyeing him dully. "You get cramps if you swim too soon after . . ."

"Then let's get into the spa."

"I told you that I don't have a bathing suit."

She would have to remind him of that. He was trying not to think about her, and now all he could picture was her naked body glistening. . . . "Then let's . . ."

"What's the matter with you, Kyle?" Toni's brow lowered as she looked across the table at him. He'd been acting so strangely during dinner. She wasn't even sure he'd been listening to anything she'd said, though he hadn't seemed to take his eyes off her for more than a few seconds. Maybe he was still preoccupied with the seminar. "Why are you so antsy? Am I *that* boring?"

"Boring?" he repeated dryly, scraping back his chair. With an exaggerated stretch, he cleared his throat. "No, it's ah . . . I just need to do something physical." Deliberately he avoided her eyes. "Sitting on the plane for three hours finally got to me, I guess."

"Well," she suggested, following him with her plate to the sink, "why don't we go for a walk then?"

Her hand was snatched up the second she put her dishes down.

"Let's go," he said, practically hauling her across the floor.

"Kyle!" Toni had hardly expected the sharp jerk he gave her arm, and she slammed right into the middle of his back. It was only by bracing herself against those rigid muscles that she kept from landing in a heap at his feet. "A walk! Not a . . ."

At the same time she had balanced herself, Kyle had turned to catch her. Finding herself smashed up against his chest now, her eyes only inches from his throat, the rest of her words suddenly forgot to come out.

Kyle's arms were around her, and she was so close that she could feel the heat of his body radiating against her. A sharp intake of breath did nothing to stabilize her already rubbery legs. His scent, that warm blend of musk and something that was unmistakably Kyle, filled her nostrils and set up a chain reaction of tremors that started at the top of her head and ended somewhere at the tip of her toes.

"Sorry," he mumbled, pulling his arms away to jam his hands into his pockets. "I take it that you weren't ready to go?"

"You never were very patient," she managed, determined to sound as casual as he looked. "And, yes, I am ready. Just as soon as we get the dishes done."

"Leave them." His instruction was tossed over

his shoulder as he headed through the living room. "Madeline can take care of them in the morning."

Taking a deep breath and telling herself quite firmly that she had felt nothing, *nothing,* just a moment ago, she followed Kyle out the front door.

When Toni awoke the next morning, she swore that she'd never go for another walk with Kyle. She had expected a nice quiet little stroll down the street. Not a four-mile marathon down the hill and back up again.

One thing was painfully clear to her as she stumbled into the shower—other than the fact that her legs ached like crazy, that is. She was definitely getting out of shape. It had only been a month since she'd abandoned her twice-weekly visits to the health club back in New York, but she had to get started on some kind of exercise program soon. Kyle had quite unnecessarily pointed out as much last night, politely suggesting that she might want to use his pool to swim laps. She didn't know which had been worse, the fact that he had suggested the very thing she had just been thinking about, or his infuriating grin as he watched her struggle up the hill after him.

A half an hour later, her hair smoothed in its usual neat knot and a pale blue turtleneck tucked into her beige wool slacks, Toni followed the smell of freshly brewed coffee into the kitchen.

Madeline—the pear-shaped little woman Toni, in a rush because she'd overslept, had literally run into on her way out the door Wednesday morning—stood at the stove stirring a pot of something that looked delicious.

"Morning." Toni smiled, tossing her wool jacket over one of the chairs at the table. She stopped and gingerly rubbed the back of her leg.

"Morning," the matronly woman returned. Her warm brown eyes crinkled in a smile as she handed Toni a steaming cup of coffee. "You look like you could use this."

Toni gratefully accepted the proffered cup. "It shows, huh?"

Madeline arched her graying eyebrows and, with an empathetic nod, turned back to the stove.

Toni figured that Kyle was already at his office. When she had worked for him, he'd always spent his Saturdays there. So it was more for the sake of conversation that she asked, "Where's Kyle?" Then, not waiting for the expected response, she added, "And what are you making? It smells wonderful."

The creases in Madeline's round face deepened with her beaming smile. "Kyle's having a party in a couple of weeks, so I thought I'd freeze up a couple batches of Swedish meatballs now and make more canapés next Saturday. I don't like having to do it all at once." She frowned at the pot, and with a shrug of her ample shoulders she dropped in a couple of cloves of garlic. "And," she continued, "Kyle's downstairs working out in the weightroom. He said I wasn't to disturb you. Guess he thought you'd want to sleep in this morning. But now that you're up, I'll go get your sheets and towels and throw 'em in the laundry."

Madeline had seemed to accept Toni's presence without question, something that had puzzled Toni until Kyle had remarked the night before that he'd told Madeline "all about her"—whatever that was supposed to mean. Toni had been too busy conserving her labored breath to ask many questions. During their little "walk" she'd let Kyle do most of the talking.

Now a perverse little smile tugged at Toni's mouth as she sipped her coffee. So Kyle wasn't at his office. That could only mean that he must be sore this morning, too, and needed to work out the cramps in *his* muscles. Serves him right, she thought, all too aware of the knots in her legs. Even her knees had cramps in them.

"Does Kyle know that you're headed out somewhere this morning?" The gray curls around Madeline's face bounced over her brow as she nodded toward Toni's jacket on the chair-back.

Toni shook her head, wondering why Madeline had even asked. It wasn't like she had to check in with Kyle before she went about her business.

Madeline had a funny look on her face as she wrung her hands on her calico apron.

"What are you doing up so early?"

At the sound of Kyle's voice, Toni glanced up. She was just about to take another sip of coffee, but the cup hung suspended in midair for one heart-stopping second before she carefully lowered it.

His large frame filled the arching doorway. A

pair of gray sweatshorts clung to his lean hips, and he had a thick white towel slung around his neck. His chest and shoulders were covered with a fine sheen of perspiration, and as he raked his fingers through his tousled hair she couldn't help but notice the hard line of his muscled biceps.

Oh, come on! she chided herself as she mumbled, "Good morning," into her cup. Just because he's half-naked and looks so . . . so *male* isn't any reason to get nervous. This is Kyle! Remember?

Kyle's eyes slid carelessly over her slender form, starting at the toes of her calfskin pumps. When his inspection reached the coil of her hair, he frowned. "You going somewhere?"

Madeline cleared her throat and dropped a metal lid into the sink.

He hadn't waited for Toni's response and was heading toward the refrigerator. The ease with which he moved, lithe sinew and muscle rippling smoothly as he covered the distance of the kitchen, told Toni that he was suffering no effect from their little jaunt last night.

"To the office," she returned, a little jealous of his effortless movements. "I'm surprised you're not at yours already."

He reached into the refrigerator and pulled out a carton of milk. "It's Saturday."

Toni stared at his broad back, wondering if she'd just missed something somewhere. "I had a friend who once told me that you can accomplish more on the weekend when the phone isn't ringing than you can otherwise all week. Don't you subscribe to that philosophy anymore?"

Over the rim of her cup, she watched him drain the tumbler of milk, then put the empty glass down on the counter.

Madeline handed him a wooden spoon. "Give the meatballs a stir in a minute," she instructed. "I'm going to put the rest of the laundry in."

"Yes, ma'am." Kyle saluted, then turned to lean against the counter. He eyed Toni levelly. "I never work on weekends. At least, not unless I have to."

That didn't sound like Kyle at all, and Toni's expression was doubtful. "You're not serious."

"Oh, yes, I am," he returned flatly. "And don't you think you deserve to take a day off?"

"What I deserve"—her mind was already on the stack of work she'd left on her desk, a deliberate effort to avoid thinking about the terribly masculine form only four feet away from her—"and what I get, are two different things."

"Want some friendly advice?"

His tone was making her a little skeptical. "That depends."

"On what?"

Her smile lacked its usual brightness. Something didn't feel quite right. "The advice."

"You're not going to like it."

She already had that feeling. But why? "Knowing you," she said, "I'm probably going to hear it anyway."

He didn't even bother acknowledging her attempt at lightness, and she was surprised at the sharpness in his tone. "You've had that office for a month, and if you'd managed your time properly, you wouldn't have to spend so much of it working now. Learn to delegate. Being a manager and a broker are two full-time jobs."

In the past Toni would have expected his criticisms, welcomed his observations. But now his reproach irritated her.

Maybe it was just because she felt so stiff and achy that the little irritation loomed so much larger. Or maybe it was because there was something about his presence that was so infuriatingly disturbing. Whatever the reason, she could feel her body growing more rigid by the second.

"Apparently you've forgotten that *you* were the one who told me that if I wanted something done right, I'd have to do it myself." Her voice was tight, an unmistakable sign of the control she was trying to exercise. Toni rarely lost her temper, and she certainly wasn't going to now. "And I do delegate," she informed him evenly. "But there are some things I don't trust anyone else with. As you so aptly pointed out, I have only been there a month and it takes time to know the people you're working with. Once I . . ."

Kyle's eyes narrowed, their glittering gray depths fixed steadily on hers. "You should know your employees by now," he cut in. "And you should be getting rid of that guy whose been causing you all that extra work. You can't do his job and yours and still expect to . . ."

"I don't think I need you to tell me how to do my job anymore." Her interruption was deliberately quiet, her expression a glacial mask.

Even with the hard glare Kyle was bestowing on her, he looked more attractive than she'd ever seen him before. So totally physical. And so aggravatingly self-confident. She was feeling more than just anger at the moment. But she didn't want to define the more threatening things he was making her feel.

Her gaze had never faltered, and she saw a dangerous flicker of certainty in his eyes. "Somebody needs to tell you," he said curtly.

"Well, you don't need to worry about it." She turned and put her cup down on the counter. Her hands were beginning to tremble, and she wasn't about to let Kyle see her slosh coffee all over the floor. She hated not being in control, and that betraying tremor only made her more upset. "I've outgrown my need for . . ." She started to say "your approval," but caught herself before the words slipped out. She didn't even know where they'd come from!

"You've outgrown your need for what, Toni?" Kyle looked only slightly less angry than she did.

The fact that he was angry at all thoroughly confused her.

Not about to admit what she'd just been thinking, she reached for the pearl at the base of her throat. Absently she ran it along its chain. "It's not important," she whispered.

Neither one of them said anything then, both choosing to stare anywhere but at each other. They had argued before, but always about ideas or ideals. Never had they argued on a personal level. Whatever it was that was going on now seemed to be more than a simple disagreement between friends.

The uncomfortable silence seemed deafening in the sunlit room.

The silence stretched on. Though she wasn't

looking at him, her gaze riveted to the toes of her shoes, she could almost feel his eyes burning through her.

When he finally spoke there was a huskiness in his voice that betrayed more than Toni was prepared to recognize. "Maybe it's important to me, princess."

A tight little lump lodged in her throat. She didn't want to admit how much those words meant to her. She didn't want them to mean anything at all! "I can't imagine why," she mumbled.

When he didn't respond, she slowly raised her eyes. He was moving toward her. When he stopped less than a foot away, it was all she could do to breathe.

More than a little intimidated by his physical presence, and upset with herself for being that way, she tipped her head back and forced a lightness into her voice that didn't want to be there. "It really doesn't matter, Kyle." Then, wanting desperately to change the subject, she asked, "Did the lecture you promised me the other night have anything to do with my less than exemplary work habits?"

"Not really," he said quietly. His expression softened as he watched her trying to regain the tiny edge she'd lost on her control a few minutes before. "We didn't get a chance to talk much last night, did we? You seemed to be spending most of your time either complaining about how steep the hill was . . . or panting."

He was obviously trying to erase the inexplicable tension that had so suddenly sprung up between them. And Toni appreciated his effort.

Wishing that he'd move—wishing that she could find the strength to move herself—she slanted him a nervy little glance. "I've never been able to carry on a conversation when it takes every ounce of breath I've got to keep my lungs from collapsing." Her gaze was involuntarily drawn to the dark hair curling against his chest. She wished she had the nerve to run her fingers through those soft, springy curls. "And the next time I suggest going for a walk, remind me how my legs feel this morning, would you?"

To her relief, he took a step back. But relief was short-lived. He was staring at the gentle contour of her breasts, rounded beneath her sweater. His eyes seemed to linger there before slowly moving down the sharp crease in her slacks.

Toni felt like she'd just been undressed by a pro.

"Your legs pretty sore?"

She nodded, trying to pretend that she hadn't noticed the way he'd been looking at her. It was difficult ignoring something so blatant, but at least he'd had the decency to *sound* sympathetic.

"I think I have permanent cramps in my calfs . . . and about a half a dozen blisters on my feet." She really didn't have any blisters. It just felt that way.

A devilish smile lit his face, and he rubbed his chin thoughtfully. "I'd be more than happy to rub them for you."

"I'll just bet you would, Donovan," she teased, determined to match his mood. She knew that he couldn't possibly be serious, but for a fleeting second she wondered what he'd do if she took him up on his offer. Then she wondered why the thought had even entered her mind. "I'm sure you have your massage technique down to an absolute science."

"Interested?" He grinned.

She managed to look completely appalled at the idea. "After the way you lit into me a few minutes ago, you'd probably start at my ankles and wind up wringing my neck. We'll just leave things the way they are. Cramps and all."

Apology and something else she couldn't quite define shadowed his otherwise playful features. "I really didn't mean to 'light into you," he said, raking his fingers through his silvering black hair. "It was just that I . . ." He gave a slight shrug, and his mischievous grin returned. "Let's get back to that massage. I've been told that I'm really quite good." He glanced over his shoulder as his housekeeper came bustling back into the room. "Madeline here's one of my biggest supporters."

Madeline? Sweet, motherly, sixtyish Madeline?

"About what?" Madeline asked, frowning at the pot. "I thought I asked you to stir these."

Sheepishly Kyle handed Madeline the spoon he'd abandoned on the counter. "I forgot. And I just offered to rub the cramps out of Toni's legs, but she doesn't trust my expertise."

It wasn't Kyle's expertise Toni mistrusted. It was herself.

"Oh, he's really quite good," Madeline

chirped, busying herself at the stove. "I've got a bad spot in my back," she waved the wooden spoon in the general direction of her shoulder blades—"right here. Any time it gets tight, all Kyle has to do is work at it for a couple of minutes and the kink's gone. I've paid chiropractors a small fortune to do what he does for nothing. If you've got a tight muscle, he'll get rid of it for you."

Toni doubted that seriously. If he so much as touched her, every muscle in her body would constrict.

Seeing Kyle's suspicious grin, Toni began moving toward the door. Retreat and run seemed to be the best course of action at the moment.

"Hold it." Kyle had snagged her arm as she reached for her jacket and was now pointing to the chair. "Sit down. It'll only take a minute."

She wasn't about to subject herself to this torture. And that's exactly what it would be. The thought of his strong hands touching her . . . "I've really got to get to work," she mumbled, struggling into her jacket.

"You aren't going to the game with Kyle?"

Toni barely had one arm in the sleeve when Madeline's question, and the feel of Kyle's hands on her shoulders, stopped her. Before she could open her mouth to protest Kyle's actions, or ask Madeline what she was talking about, Toni had been pushed down into the chair.

"She doesn't have time today." Kyle's words were directed to Madeline as he lowered himself to the floor at Toni's feet. "It takes a while to get organized when you take over an office. And it's easier to get your paperwork done when you don't have a dozen people around asking a bunch of questions. We'll try for the game next weekend." He tipped his head back and met Toni's blank expression. "Pull your pant leg up."

She just sat there and crossed her arms over her chest.

Had he actually defended her to Madeline with the same argument he'd used against her not ten minutes ago? Was he really going to massage her legs? What game?

Seeing that she wasn't going to cooperate, Kyle shrugged and slipped his hands beneath the hem of her slacks. In one smooth movement, he bunched the fabric around her knee, then proceeded to do the same with the other.

Toni's eyes widened.

Kyle's mouth curled in a satisfied smirk.

Madeline started humming to herself.

"You probably should have sat in the spa for a while when we got home last night," Kyle said to Toni. His hands cupped her left calf, and he was kneading the knotted muscle with gentle, rhythmic motions. "The heat would have soaked some of the soreness out. Oh, Madeline"—He continued his businesslike massage, never missing a stroke, which was what Toni felt like she was about to have, and little tingles were racing madly from her toes to her thighs—"that cocktail party I'm having in a couple of weeks? There's another eight people coming, so be sure to fix enough food. And I'll be bringing a few of the guys back here after the game today."

"Don't worry about the party," Madeline returned, busily chopping an onion. "I'll put some sandwiches together and leave them in the fridge before I go."

Kyle may have been talking to his housekeeper, but his eyes were following his hands. One of them slipped up behind Toni's knee then traced a too-light path down to her ankle. "Nice legs," he mumbled under his breath, then spoke to Madeline again. "Since I'll be home all of next week . . ."

The easy banter between Kyle and the woman who seemed more like a dear aunt than a housekeeper continued. But Toni was hearing little of it. He might as well have been kneading bread for all the attention he was paying to Toni. Toni, on the other hand, was aware of nothing but Kyle and the way his long fingers alternately punished and then caressed her soft skin. He slipped her shoe off, still talking to Madeline, and began working the pads of his fingers in small circles over the sole of her foot.

The knots in her legs were slowly dissolving, but the one in her stomach wasn't. She hugged her arms tighter around her middle, her eyes glued to the top of his dark head. The towel still hung around the corded muscles of his neck, and the morning sun slanting through the skylight made his shoulders look like hammered bronze.

Kyle had repositioned himself and was now sitting cross-legged on the floor. He laid her foot against his thigh, working methodically on each of her toes.

The chaos he was creating with her senses

had made it impossible for her to speak. The tightness in her throat seemed to be building in less specific places.

This is all perfectly innocent, she told herself, and tried to ignore the tingling that had spread through her whole body. "What . . ." She cleared her throat and tried again. "What game are you two talking about?"

Kyle pulled her other foot onto his lap and began massaging her other calf. "A bunch of us guys get together on Saturdays to play football. That's all." His kneading now resembled more of a caress. "You used to work with some of them—Jerry Andrews, Todd Ruger. They bring their families sometimes. I just thought you'd like to see them again. You'll see 'em at the party though."

"You mean I'm invited?" Why did her voice sound so husky?

He glanced up at her, his gray eyes narrowed. "Of course you are. You'll know half the people there anyway, and they'd shoot me if you didn't show up."

"What's the party for?"

"Carol Gray's being transferred to Denver. It's sort of a combination promotion-farewell party."

Toni barely knew Carol. She had joined Kyle's company just before Toni left, and at the moment, Toni was hard pressed to remember what the woman even looked like.

Wanting a diversion, any diversion, Toni tried to formulate some conversational question about Carol. But what Kyle was doing now stopped her cold.

His index finger lay lightly on her kneecap.

Slowly, he traced a feathery path over the curve and down her shin. Reaching her ankle, he shackled it in the loop formed by his finger and thumb. Her ankle looked so tiny compared to his large hands.

The strange intensity in his expression vanished with his lopsided grin. "That wasn't so bad now. Was it?" Giving her calf a squeeze, he pulled himself to his feet. "And in return for that favor, I'd like you to do me one." He caught the ends of his towel with both hands, drawing it tighter over the back of his neck. "Wear a dress to that party. You really do have a great pair of legs, Collins."

With that, he strolled out of the kitchen, calling back to Madeline that he'd be leaving right after he took his shower.

Toni shoved her pant legs back down and took a couple of deep breaths. Forcing herself to think of nothing other than the mechanics of putting herself back together, she slipped her shoes on and smoothed the lapels of her jacket. One thing she'd never been very good at was blanking her mind. She tried, but her rational brain was working furiously to overcome the assault of less logical thought. She felt a little shaky because she needed another cup of coffee. The only reason she was flustered was because she was already behind schedule. The heated points of fire that still burned her legs where Kyle had caressed them were just muscle cramps. And Kyle had just been his usual omnipotent, teasing and exasperating self. All good, sound, rational . . . excuses.

"Well," she said to Madeline, enormously

pleased with her split-second analysis. "I
. . . ah, guess I'd better get to the office and
see if I can get something accomplished."

"Oh," Madeline smiled gently, drawing the
word out a little. "I'd say that quite a bit's been
accomplished already."

The cherubic little woman turned back to her
task, completely ignoring Toni's puzzled frown.

Chapter Three

𝒦yle glanced down at the raven-haired woman whose fingers were deftly working at the knot in his tie. Her warm lips were pressed to the side of his neck, working an expert pattern upward to nibble seductively at his ear.

Why couldn't he respond to her? Maggie had always excited him before. So what was wrong now?

Muttering an inaudible profanity to himself, he took Maggie by the shoulders and gently pushed her away. He grabbed his snifter of brandy from the coffee table. Wanting only to end this ridiculous charade, he stood up.

Confusion was reflected in the woman's huge brown eyes. Her hair was tousled, but Kyle thought that it just looked messy rather than beguiling. Instead of finding the results of his handiwork provocative—her slightly smeared lipstick and the swell of her full breasts revealed by her unbuttoned blouse—he felt only disgust with himself. And oddly empty.

Maggie tugged at her skirt as she rose from the sofa, not bothering to fasten her top. "What's the matter?" she asked sulkily. "You seem a little preoccupied tonight."

She reached for his arm, but he moved away before she could touch him.

His jaw clenched tightly as he stood at the mantel, pretending interest in a small figurine.

A little preoccupied was a gross understatement. Ever since he'd returned from Chicago, he'd been able to think of nothing but Toni. Toni leaning against the kitchen counter, her hair wrapped in a towel and wearing that soft blue robe and still sleepy-eyed as she drank her morning coffee. Toni as she rushed past him an hour later, looking every inch the no-nonsense executive in her severely tailored suit. Toni teasing him while he tried to help her when it was her turn to cook dinner. Toni frowning in concentration as she sat at the table with the files she always brought home from the office.

He'd offered to go house-hunting with her on Sunday, wanting nothing more than to spend the day with her. But she'd just leveled those beautiful blue eyes at him and said that she already had plans to go with Greg. Kyle had been quite pleased with his bantering comment about "going after the rich doctor," though something very unpleasant had twisted inside him.

It couldn't possibly have been jealousy.

She had certainly done nothing to encourage

anything other than the friendship they already shared. And Kyle was trying desperately to act the same way he always had toward her. He had become obsessed with the thought of her, though. He wished that it had been Toni's lips that had so passionately returned his kisses just a short while ago. Did she touch Greg the way Maggie . . . ?

That uncomfortable knot constricted in his gut again. Thinking about Toni in another man's arms was doing nothing for his mood. His inability to respond to Maggie had put him in a lousy frame of mind, and hadn't done a thing for his ego.

Cripe! he thought, raking his fingers through his hair. Here I am with a gorgeous woman who wants nothing more than for me to take her to bed, and I'm as limp as hay after a rainstorm. What in the hell are you doing to me, Toni?

Glancing over at the beautiful foreign correspondent he'd been seeing off and on for the past several months, a self-deprecating smile hung on his lips. Maggie Sherman was worldly and sophisticated. And, more importantly, no more interested in a commitment than he was.

"Sorry, Maggie," he said, draining his brandy. He handed her the empty snifter and dropped a quick kiss on her forehead. "I know I've been rotten company tonight. Give me a call when you get back from wherever it is you're off to this time, and I'll make it up to you."

Kyle wasn't accustomed to walking away from a willing woman. He couldn't believe that he was doing it now.

It was well past midnight when Kyle slid his key into the lock and pushed open his front door. The lights in the living room were on, but the house was quiet. Toni was probably already asleep.

She was. But not in her bed. Kyle's hand stilled as he reached over to turn out the table lamp, his eyes frozen on her sleeping form.

She was lying on the sofa, one arm curled beneath her head and the other still grasping the edge of the *Wall Street Journal,* which had fallen partway to the floor.

Kyle's eyes moved slowly from the thick lashes brushing her cheeks, then to her softly parted mouth. Taking advantage of her oblivion, his eyes moved measuringly down the length of her body.

Beneath her silky white caftan the tantalizing swell of her tiny breasts rose and fell with her rhythmic breathing. The slenderness of her hips was revealed by the loose folds of the satiny fabric, and her long legs were bent slightly, betraying their lithe shapeliness. He remembered well the feel of her skin when she'd reluctantly submitted to his massage the other morning.

A glint of self-mockery slipped into his eyes. The shower he'd been in such a hurry to take then had been a cold one. He'd nearly turned blue waiting for the feelings she'd unknowingly elicited to go away. Feelings that were being resurrected now.

His gaze traced its path back to her serene features. Sleep erased the unfamiliar aggressiveness he saw when she was awake. Now she looked more like the innocent snow princess he'd once known. But she wasn't an innocent anymore, he reminded himself, recalling the conversation they'd had when he'd met her at the University Club. He didn't know why that disappointed him so. Maybe it was just that he hated the thought of her becoming like Maggie— like all the other women he associated with.

Why did it hurt to know that he'd lost something he'd always told himself he never wanted?

The dull ache that had formed in his loins escalated to a demanding throb. He drew in a shuddering breath and clenched his hands. He had no idea how she would react, what damage he might do. But his need to touch her—just touch her—was overriding logic.

Slowly his hand moved toward her cheek.

Toni's last conscious thought had been of Kyle. More specifically, the status of their renewed friendship. The ease with which they had settled into each other's life surprised her. And every day she forcibly reminded herself that she must think of him as nothing but a brother.

He barely resembled the man she thought she'd once known. A lot of his old cynicism was gone, yet she still sensed a remoteness that she wished she could understand. She also wished she could understand why she couldn't stop thinking about him. Her thoughts had a way of drifting into very dangerous territory, and her dreams weren't helping much either.

Something warm and feather-light trailed over her cheek. The sensation was pleasant, and in her dreams she imagined Kyle gently moving the tip of his finger over the fullness of her bottom lip. So many times she'd fallen asleep wondering what it would be like, just once, to feel his lips against hers.

"Oh, princess," she heard a deep voice whisper. A faint flutter of breath seemed to touch her forehead.

She knew she was dreaming. Just as she was dreaming that Kyle's fingers were tenderly pulling the pins from her hair and laying the heavy waist-length mass over her shoulders, smoothing the corn-silk-colored tresses along her arms.

It was a wonderful dream. Kyle was lifting her, cradling her slender form against the solid wall of his chest. She could almost feel those strong arms holding her so tightly, his unhurried movements as he carried her away.

Her head lay against the smooth cotton of his shirt, her hair cascading over his arm. Her breath mingled with the faint scent of brandy and spicy clean musk. She could hear his heart beating a little too rapidly, and her hand seemed to move to where it echoed in his chest. He felt warm and she snuggled deeper against him.

Not wanting to break the illusion, she fought the thick fog of sleep. Strange sensations kept intruding though, and her eyes fluttered open.

This was far too real to be a product of her imagination. But it was also impossible to comprehend what she was seeing.

For a moment, those floating images tried unsuccessfully to meld with reality. Then senses sharpened. She was staring at black curls emerging from an open collar, and she could see the tiny pulse beating at the base of his neck.

This was no dream.

Kyle *was* holding her.

And he was standing in the hall between their bedrooms.

The situation was incomprehensible. Her greeting sounded ridiculous. All she could manage was a very bewildered, "Hi."

There was a fair amount of hesitation reflected in Kyle's shadowed features. "Hi, yourself," he said quietly. Then, not moving a muscle, he added, "I suppose you wonder what I'm doing?"

Through the thin fabric of her caftan, she could feel the heat of his hard body. She was also aware of the fact that he was making no effort to put her down. "The thought had occurred to me," she replied, almost certain that she must still be sleeping.

Something else just occurred to her. Her hair was no longer in its usual coil. Kyle *had* taken it down. She hadn't just imagined it after all. Had the slight pressure she'd felt on her cheek and on her lips also been real? She'd thought it had just been his fingers trailing so lightly, but . . . "Kyle?"

"Hmmm?"

"Did you . . . ?" Her voice, still thick with sleep, faltered. Why couldn't she just ask? If he'd kissed her, she wanted to know it. But if he hadn't, she'd feel like a fool for asking.

"Did I what?"

Deciding that the question was no more foolish than the fact that they were carrying on a conversation with him holding her like some maiden he was in the process of rescuing, she drew in a preparatory breath. She hadn't made a fool of herself in a long time. Undoubtedly, she was due. "Did you kiss me?"

His lips parted slightly, and his chest expanded against her as he drew in a lungful of air. The motion crushed her breast tighter, and it was impossible to tell whose heartbeat had just increased the most. "No," he said, the mysterious depths of his smoky gray eyes revealing nothing. The lines bracketing his mouth seemed to deepen as he studied her closely. "Not yet."

"Not . . . yet?" Was he implying that he planned on doing just that? Certainly she must still be dreaming.

He watched the myriad of emotions play over her flushed face, and the corners of his mouth tilted upward. "I was definitely tempted, but I thought I'd wait until you were awake. That way you'd have a chance to tell me off."

She couldn't begin to fathom what he was talking about. Why would she want to tell him off? Obviously some critical part of her brain was refusing to function.

Catching the faint scent of brandy suddenly put everything into perspective. So *that's* why he was acting like this. "You've been drinking," she accused flatly. She should have known that only something like being under the influence would make him notice her as something other than his buddy.

"A little," he admitted, moving the arm supporting her back up a bit. He'd had a glass of wine with dinner and then the brandy at Maggie's. But he was far from being affected. "And to answer the question you're about to ask . . . yes, I know what I'm doing."

Toni seriously doubted that. He didn't look or sound drunk. But he had to be to be acting like this. "Put me down," she ordered mildly, "and I'll go fix you some coffee."

"I don't want any coffee."

"Then let me go get you some aspirin."

"I don't need any aspirin."

"Well, put me down anyway!"

"Why?"

"Kyle!"

The slightly frantic note in her voice had more to do with the way her body insisted on reacting to his than any great desire to be released by those strong arms. It didn't make any sense. But at the moment, nothing did. Least of all Kyle.

When he'd repositioned his arm behind her back a moment ago, his hand had come precariously close to her breast. That hand now moved upward, and she could feel it lying just below the fullness.

Willing herself to sound calmer than she felt, she repeated her request that he put her down.

This time, he complied.

Releasing his arm from beneath her knees, he let her legs slip to the floor. The arm around her back stayed right where it was, holding her loosely against him.

Tilting her head back, her white gold hair tumbling down her arms, she flattened her hands against his chest and gave him a tentative shove.

He didn't budge.

"Look," she began, wondering if she'd misjudged the situation. Maybe he hadn't had too much to drink. Maybe he did know exactly what he was doing. Immediately she dismissed her doubts. He wasn't drunk, but he had to be at least slightly inebriated. "I really think you need some coffee."

His clear gray eyes clouded, and she felt the pressure of his arm around her waist lighten. "You don't want me to kiss you, do you?"

There was a certainty in his words that made them a statement, not a question. And beneath that certainty was a touch of disappointment. Was it disappointment she was seeing in his otherwise shuttered expression?

Despite the hard set to his jaw, he looked terribly vulnerable. She had never known Kyle to look anything but completely unaffected.

Her first assessment had to be right. Hard telling how much he'd had to drink to allow her to see that.

Neither one of them had moved. Toni held his gaze steadily.

This was her chance. He was handing her an opportunity she couldn't pass up. If he kissed her, she wouldn't have to wonder anymore if bells would go off in her head like she'd always heard they would. Toni had never heard bells in all of her twenty-seven years. Faint tinkles. But never bells.

She could feel the tension in Kyle's body. From

the stillness of his features, she knew that he was waiting. The next move had to be hers.

A thousand little uncertainties skittered through her brain. But she shoved them away. Her bottom lip was caught between her teeth as she hesitantly curved her arms around his neck.

Her fingers brushed the silky black hair above his collar. Delighting in its crisp, clean feel, she moved her fingers upward through its softness. Her hand cupped the back of his head.

Kyle's eyes widened slightly, but he didn't move.

She hoped that they were good enough friends to withstand this little experiment.

Feeling his hard body aligned so intimately to hers was already causing her to have second thoughts. She was going to be practical about this though. Telling herself that she probably wouldn't react any differently to Kyle's kiss than she had to any other man's, she leaned a little closer. It might be pleasant, or just interesting. Or maybe she wouldn't feel anything at all.

The tingle that had started in her breasts and was spreading downward told her that the latter wouldn't be the case.

"Yes," she whispered. "I do want you to kiss me."

For a moment, she thought that he hadn't heard her. Or that what she'd said hadn't registered. But then she felt his hand wending through the heavy hair at the nape of her neck.

In his eyes she could see a question, and desire.

"You sure?" His voice was deep, threaded with

a huskiness that made the quietly spoken words deliciously intimate.

"Yes," she returned, not even sure that any sound had passed the knot in her throat.

With a gentle tug, he tipped her head back and brushed his lips against her softly parted mouth.

His touch was firm and cool, and a little like brandy-scented velvet. Increasing the pressure a little, he coaxed her bottom lip down with the tip of his tongue, but took no advantage of the entrance she had just allowed him. Slowly he traced the outline of her mouth, savoring its delicate texture.

Toni felt her fingers clutching the steely cords of his neck, drawing him closer. Just when she thought he would deepen the contact, allow her to taste the warmth she so suddenly craved, he lifted his head.

His fingers tightened in her hair, and there was no mistaking the unveiled need in his questioning eyes.

It wasn't enough. "Again," she breathed, already aware of an odd heat radiating through her.

There was nothing tentative about the way he claimed her this time. His tongue slipped inside her mouth, tangling with the sweet warmth of her own. Teasing, seducing.

The romantics had lied. It wasn't bells she heard. It was a rushing sound, like her blood pressure had just reached its absolute limit. Sensations more exquisite than she'd ever known coursed through her, enlivening nerves that burned in foreign places. Forgetting everything but the man drawing her into that mindless whirl of feeling, she allowed her body to flow against him, her soft curves molding to his hard planes.

His hand was pressing into the small of her back, urging her to feel the extent of his arousal. As his hips tilted forward, tantalizing his rigidity against her stomach, she twisted against him, unconsciously imitating the motion he was teaching her.

The low moan that made its way past the rushing in her ears could have been his, or hers. She couldn't tell. Nothing mattered except the feel of him. No matter how well she knew the reasons why he was so wrong for her, she had just passed the invisible line she had drawn for herself.

He had only wanted to touch her. To hold her. And taste that beautifully seductive mouth. But the feel of her—the gentle roundness of the small breasts his fingers ached to caress, the sleek line of her back where his hand moved in slow, deep circles—was even more fantastic than he had imagined. Even more incredible was that she had invited the kiss he'd been so certain she didn't want.

Though he could sense her willingness, she had taken no further initiative. Her hands hadn't moved from where they clutched him so tightly. He wanted to feel those slender hands roaming over his body, to feel her lips on his neck, his chest.

He wanted more than that.

He wanted to part those long legs and bury

himself in the moist heat he knew he'd find there. To feel her surround him and forget for a while the emptiness that could never be filled. He could never have what he wanted, what most men took for granted.

Kyle knew that he wasn't being fair—to either one of them. If this were anyone but Toni . . .

Desire erased conscious thought. Never had he ached so badly to possess a woman.

There had been a certain shyness in Toni's touch. But Kyle didn't acknowledge it. Convinced that she knew exactly what she was doing with that sweet tongue of hers, he didn't doubt for a minute that she possessed the knowledge to drive a man out of his mind. Toni always put her heart and soul into everything she did. He was certain that her skills as a lover had been perfected with that same passion.

Gently lifting the weight of her breast, his thumb rolling over the hardened nipple, he trailed a line of hot kisses down the arched column of her throat. She tasted so good. So good.

"Perfect," he rasped, his palm folding over the gentle fullness. "So firm, and so perfect." Her rigid bud burned against his hand, the point growing harder as he pressed the thin fabric of her caftan against it in a slow, erotic circle.

A tiny gasp lodged where his lips pressed at the cleft between her breasts. Something warm and liquid had coiled in her stomach—a feeling so intense that Toni couldn't even identify it. Unprepared for the torrent of sensation Kyle was eliciting, she tried to fight the sensual web tangling about her. It was a half-hearted struggle, and she lost. Though he had just been given the total extent of her knowledge, she knew that he wanted more—that she wanted to give more. But he would have to tell her how.

His lips had found her mouth again, his drugging kiss silencing the words screaming in her mind. *Please, Kyle. Show me how to love you.* Cool air brushed over her heated skin as he slid the fabric from her shoulder. His tongue ceased its plunging, allowing her mute pleas to be heard. "Kyle," she breathed, shivering as he trailed moist kisses along her collarbone, "I don't . . ." The words she needed to say simply couldn't come out. *I don't know what to do. Tell me how to please you.*

The tension she could feel rippling through the muscles of his thighs where they pressed against hers and in the well-defined contours of his back where her hands now caressed him suddenly grew more pronounced. It wasn't the tension of sexual excitement, but the tautness of anxiety. Kyle had grown still.

Toni froze, her own body turning to stone in the circle of his arms.

She felt his heavy breath at her temple and the whisper of silk covering her shoulder. Slowly, holding her breath, she withdrew her arms.

Kyle's words were barely audible, but they seemed to echo off the walls of the dimly lit hall. "I must be insane."

His arms fell away, and Toni took a faltering step back.

Without the support of his body, it was all she

could do to keep from sagging against the wall behind her. She felt weak and confused. Terribly confused.

Kyle cupped his hand over the back of his neck, rotating his head as if to ease his tension, and let out a long, low breath. It was several tense seconds before he looked back over at Toni. And even then, all he said was, "Sorry."

Never had she heard so much disappointment conveyed in one word. But who was he disappointed with? Himself? Her?

"Don't be," she returned, determined to defuse the whole inexplicable situation. The best thing to do, she decided, amazed that her mind was functioning at all, was to pretend as though it hadn't mattered. It had been nothing more than a simple, experimental kiss between friends.

Simple? The words rumbled dumbly in her mind. Hardly! But she wasn't going to argue semantics with herself at the moment. "You're going to have an awful headache in the morning." She tried her best to sound teasing. "And you're right about being insane. Alcohol can make some people a little crazy."

That explanation might work for him. But what about her? She didn't have any convenient excuses to fall back on.

Kyle's dark eyebrows lowered sharply. "What are you talking about?"

Drawing in a decidedly unsteady breath, she crossed her arms over her still-taut breasts. Never had she felt so . . . so tense. "It's obvious that you had a little too much to drink," she chided gently, trying to keep all of her insecurities at bay. Rejection never did much for a person's confidence. "You know you wouldn't have kissed me if you'd been sober."

She'd give anything if he'd just smile. Even a little. She tried to encourage him with one of her own.

It didn't work. The way he was looking at her made her wonder if she'd just grown antlers or something. He didn't look confused now. Incredulous seemed more like it.

"You mean you think I'm drunk?"

"I didn't say you were drunk . . . exactly." To Toni, the total disbelief plastered on his face resembled a vague, alcoholic haze. And he did seem a little disoriented. "I just said it's obvious that . . ." It didn't seem worth repeating, and another thought had just occurred to her. He'd seemed curiously hesitant about keeping the date he'd had tonight. "Did something go wrong with your date? I really didn't think you'd be home until . . ." She had started to say "in the morning," but finished with "later."

"My date?" he repeated. "Oh, yeah," he added quickly, grasping at the excuse he'd just been offered. "Maggie was that 'little situation' I'd mentioned before, and things . . . well . . ." He was lying through his teeth. There had never been anything except sex between him and Maggie. That didn't even exist anymore. And the "little situation" he'd referred to earlier had been nothing more than a joking reference to having Toni live with him. He'd meant nothing by those words—then.

Toni knew that she should offer her sympathy, tell him she was sorry that things hadn't gone well with his date. But she couldn't. Kyle didn't seem particularly upset about Maggie, and the memory of his kisses still burned too feverishly in Toni's mind for her to be charitable about another woman's loss.

"You'd better get to bed," Kyle said, suddenly looking very tired. "You said you had to meet the good doctor before his rounds in the morning."

Toni told herself that she only imagined the slight derision in Kyle's voice. She hadn't bothered to tell him that all those "dates" she had with Greg to go house-hunting were really expeditions to find investment property for Greg and his associates at his clinic. She'd yet to try to find a house for herself—she simply hadn't had time—and she and Greg had quickly come to the understanding that they shared nothing more than a few common interests.

This *is* crazy, she told herself, not even aware that she was shaking her head. Or that Kyle was in the process of unbuttoning his shirt. She was looking down at the soft gray carpet, digging her bare toes into the nap. Here we are, standing in the hall in the middle of the night discussing another man and another woman and not three minutes ago we were . . . She glanced up then, and immediately wished she hadn't. Kyle was shrugging out of his shirt. "I'd take some aspirin if I were you," she mumbled, quickly stepping inside her bedroom. Closing the door, she added a hasty, " 'Night, Kyle."

All the while they had been talking, she'd been painfully aware of the savage pounding in her chest. Even now, safely away from him, it seemed to take forever for her heart to resume a more even beat. It wasn't until she could trust her legs to carry her to her bed that she finally moved from where she'd flattened herself against the door.

She'd tried not to let it happen. But it had. During the past few days she'd found many of the old feelings creeping back, along with some frightening new ones—feelings she had firmly told herself didn't exist.

There was no denying their existence now. She had fallen in love with Kyle all over again. Only this time, it wasn't the naive hero-worship that had made her think that everything he did or said was beyond scrutiny. It was the kind of caring born of true friendship. A knowledge that recognized all Kyle's little imperfections and loved him in spite of them.

How could it have happened so fast? It had only been ten days!

Toni undressed and pulled on the very un-sexy pink flowered nightgown her mother had sent her last Christmas from London. Or had it been Ireland? She couldn't remember, and right now the path of her mother's constant jaunts was the last thing on her mind. Toni shoved the hair out of her eyes and plopped down on the bed.

Of all the men in the world, why did she have to be in love with a man who viewed marriage with such distaste and all but broke out in hives when anyone even mentioned children?

She snapped off the light and slid between the covers. That kind of thinking was far too premature, and quite out-dated. In most respects she was very much a liberated and forward-thinking individual. She was also an adult, and she'd face this little situation as any other red-blooded American woman would.

He had wanted her. She had felt his need, and the desire that mirrored her own had been very, very real. Doubts marred the heady knowledge that Kyle had finally noticed her as a woman. Had he sensed her inexperience? Is that why he had pulled away from her? What hadn't she done?

"Oh, hell," she mumbled, stuffing her head under her pillow. She was excited and uncertain, and in love. And there were just too many questions she couldn't answer right now. "Just pretend you're Scarlett O'Hara and think about it tomorrow."

That was the most practical thought she'd had in the last half hour. But it was a ploy that she knew wasn't going to work.

Another move like that, Donovan, Kyle chided himself as he tossed his wadded-up shirt on the chair and moved through the living room to the wet bar, and she'll move out of here so fast . . .

He didn't allow himself to complete the uncomfortable thought and, cradling his drink between his hands, sank to the sofa with a disgusted sigh. It probably would have been smarter to do about a hundred and fifty laps in the pool. But drowning himself in liquor seemed more appropriate. Toni had thought he'd had too much to drink already!

He didn't know whether to laugh at the absurdity of the situation, or just be grateful that she'd so generously excused his actions.

It had taken several seconds for her trembling plea to register. And though she hadn't said all the words, Kyle had heard the ones he thought she'd left unsaid. *I don't . . . want this!*

There had been no mistaking the desire he'd felt in her, but he was convinced now that it had been nothing more than a product of vulnerability. A woman was at her weakest when she first woke up, he told himself with unequivocal male certainty. And he had no doubt caught her with her defenses, and judgment, fogged by sleep.

It was obvious enough—when she'd finally regained her senses—that she wasn't interested in altering their relationship. So quickly had she reverted to her usual, half-teasing, half-mocking self. And then she'd asked him about his date!

He glared at the drink he'd yet to touch and shoved it across the coffee table. He had no intention of drinking himself into oblivion, though the thought had had a few nebulous merits. He felt bad enough right now without a hangover in the morning to remind him of his stupidity.

In the morning. He'd have to face her in the morning. How would she react to him?

"Knowing Toni," he muttered to himself, "I bet she'll either tease you about it, or ask you what in the hell you thought you were doing."

If she chose the latter, he had no idea how he'd respond.

All he knew at the moment was that he had to

stick to the decision he'd made days ago. He could offer her nothing more than an affair anyway, so he'd do everything in his power to see that their relationship remained just as it was. They were friends. Period.

He could learn to live with cold showers.

Chapter Four

*F*our A.M. always came too early. Anyone up at this hour either had to be crazy, or a stockbroker. Toni wondered absently if they weren't one and the same.

Leaning against the counter by the sink, she raised her hand to cover a yawn and waited for the coffee to finish brewing. She could stumble through her shower without being fully awake, but putting on makeup and getting dressed required a greater level of consciousness.

Though Toni was still fighting her usual early-morning inertia, she was aware of the sound of Kyle's shower running in his bathroom. As long as she could hear that, there was no danger of seeing him. And she didn't want to see him until she had a full grip on her mental faculties. It was very important that she be able to measure his reaction to her this morning.

Deciding that the coffemaker could complete its function without her bleary-eyed supervision, she turned to the window over the sink. It was pitch black outside and, other than a few raindrops tracing watery paths down the glass, she could see nothing but her own reflection blinking back at her.

There was no marked difference in the familiar features. Nothing to indicate that anything drastic had changed within her. A woman in love was supposed to look radiant. Or did that adage apply to a pregnant woman? It hardly mattered. No one could look radiant at four o'clock in the morning.

Toni shoved the towel, wrapped turban-style around her head, back a bit. Maybe she'd find some changes there—like gray hair.

Her silver blond hair still appeared to be the same shade it had always been. It would be almost impossible to detect any gray in it anyway. All of the changes were inside. The feelings that made her anxious and . . .

Oh, come on! her mind yawned. Be practical about this. You've got more sense than to fall in love with him, and one lousy kiss shouldn't make any . . .

"Coffee ready?"

What normally took her at least two cups of liquid caffeine to accomplish, Kyle had done in less than two seconds. Full consciousness returned with a thudding jolt.

He had stopped in the middle of the kitchen. In the mirrorlike window, she could see him briskly rubbing a towel over the back of his still-damp hair. Though his reflection was cut off at the waist, she knew that the maroon velour robe he was wearing ended above his knees—which was where she focused when she turned around.

"I . . . ah . . . think so," she mumbled, mentally kicking herself for being so preoccupied that she'd forgotten to listen for his shower.

She watched his bare feet carry him to the counter, then heard a cupboard door close and the sound of coffee being poured into mugs.

Kyle had the disgusting habit of waking up fully alert, but Toni's predawn incoherency usually allowed for only the most basic of exchanges. She hoped that his silence now was only because he wasn't expecting anything more than her customary, unintelligible mutterings. So far, she was running true to form.

Of course, there was always the possibility that he was too tired to talk this morning. It had been awfully late when he'd gotten home last night. Or maybe he's . . .

Toni cut her rationalization off with a sharp, silent admonishment and, giving the belt of her robe a tightening jerk, moved to the refrigerator. Why conjure up excuses for his silence? He hadn't had a chance to say much of anything anyway!

"How's your head this morning?" she ventured, taking a carton of cream from the shelf. She fully expected him to have a hangover. That in itself should be ample reminder of what had happened in the hallway outside their bedrooms.

Cautiously glancing up, she saw him push one of the mugs toward her. It was hard to tell if it was her question, or the fact that she'd been able to put together a comprehensible sentence at this hour, that made his dark eyebrows pinch together.

The towel he'd been drying his hair with was draped around his neck, and there was a little nick in his chin where he'd cut himself shaving. She thought she saw the muscle beneath that tiny cut jump.

"My head's fine," he replied, eyeing the carton she held in her hand. He raised his mug to his lips, watching her blandly over the rim. "When did you start drinking cream in your coffee?"

Toni's eyes jerked to the container she was opening. The deeper levels of her mind had still been wrestling with the impracticality of being in love with Kyle while her heart had been telling her to ignore that logic. Obviously she didn't function well when forced, before she had her coffee, to deal with profound thoughts—and the more conscious ones caused by the extremely disturbing impact he was having on her nerves.

I don't use cream, she thought dumbly, also telling herself that she'd better start paying more attention to her own reactions and a little less to his nonexistent ones. "This morning," she finally responded, and poured a liberal amount of cream into her mug. "I need the calcium."

She couldn't tell for sure, but it looked like there was a faint flicker of amusement in his deep gray eyes. Kyle said nothing though, and taking his mug with him, he walked out of the kitchen.

Toni let out a long, low breath and scowled down at her coffee. "How positively unenlightening," she muttered.

She didn't know what she had expected anyway. An apology? A passionate good-morning kiss? As far as she could tell, Kyle didn't seem particularly concerned about what had happened—if he remembered it at all.

That last thought wasn't very flattering.

By the time they had finished dinner the next evening, it was obvious that the incident in the hallway had been relegated to the land of the never-mentioned. It was also apparent that Kyle hadn't forgotten the unexpected physical explosion that had passed between them. Their conversations had been easy, quite companionable actually. But some enervating tension seemed to strain their intermittent silences.

It was during those silences that Toni found herself glancing guardedly toward him. And every time, she would find him watching her, a telling darkness narrowing his eyes. But all he would do was either give her a noncommittal smile, or look blankly away. The desire he would shutter so quickly was encouraging—and more than a little frustrating.

The attraction was definitely there, but it didn't look like he was going to do a thing about it. If anything, he was going out of his way *not* to touch her.

Toni, being her usual, practical self, decided that there was only one thing she could do. She hadn't imagined Kyle's response to her caresses any more than she had imagined her own to his.

It wasn't carved in stone that the male had to be the aggressor, so why shouldn't she be the one to make the move? She could handle an affair with him, couldn't she?

Toni was omitting one very important detail from her mental questioning. The only thing allowing her to think this way was the fact that she was hopelessly in love with him—practical or not. If she were honest with herself, she'd have to admit that she'd probably been in love with him for the past five years. And Someone Up There was giving her a second chance.

There was only one tiny little problem. Toni had never seduced a man before, and she wasn't quite sure how to go about it.

The most obvious place to pick up that kind of information was from a pro, of course. And who knew the art of seduction better than Kyle? She'd never hesitated to ask his advice before. So why not get a few pointers from the expert?

Toni closed the file she'd been all but ignoring for the past half hour and slanted a glance through her lashes at Kyle.

He was lying on the sofa reading the evening paper. From where she was sitting on the opposite side of the living room, she could see only his long, denim-covered legs and his fingers grasping the edges of the paper. Outside the pool of light from the table lamp beside him, mobile shadows moved on the wall from the flickering light of the fireplace. And she could hear the rain being thrown in windy gusts against the wide glass doors behind her.

It should have been a scene of absolute serenity. And it might have been except for that indefinable tension that seemed to fill the room. It made the air feel about as thick as one of Madeline's stews.

"Kyle?" Toni began, glancing down at the file resting on her knees. "Are you up to giving me a little friendly advice?"

Absently she flicked at the metal tab holding the papers in the folder. She had to appear as nonchalant as possible.

The newspaper rustled as he turned the page. "Sure. You having a problem with investment strategy or something?"

"It's a strategy problem, but it's something of a more personal nature."

"And you want my advice?"

Was there a thread of strain in his voice? "Well, since you're a male, I thought you'd be the most logical person to ask." When he didn't say anything, and the paper didn't move, she continued casually. "There's this man that I'd like to get to know better, and he's being a little . . . well, I guess you'd call it 'reserved.' I thought maybe you could . . ."

"Who?" The voice behind the newspaper sounded choked.

"Oh, his name's not important," she returned innocently. "I just thought you could tell me how to thaw him out. I think he likes me, but we can't seem to get past the . . . past the hand-holding stage." Well, she justified to herself, he did hold my hand once. Sort of.

She wished she could see his face. On the other hand, it was probably better that she couldn't. With him hiding behind the paper, he couldn't see hers either.

"Just how far do you want to go with this guy?"

Point-blank. That had always been Kyle's style.

She gave the metal tab another flick. "As far as I can get." Her bright blue eyes shot to the white-knuckled hand holding the paper, and she swallowed a disbelieving moan. Did she actually say what she thought she had?

Kyle's voice sounded a little tight. "I suppose you could always try plying him with alcohol. That should loosen his inhibitions."

It did . . . once, she thought dryly. "I'd prefer him sober."

"Then how about a quiet dinner by candlelight?"

They had dinner together almost every night, and Toni had the feeling that a couple of candles wouldn't make any difference. "I need something better than that. Something more . . ."

"Obvious?" came the voice from behind the paper.

"Well, nothing *overt*," she countered, picking up her pen to draw little squiggles on the folder. "Just tell me what appeals to a man who . . ."

Kyle noisely turned another page and gave the paper an impatient snap. "I can't believe that any man could possibly be that dense. If you like him, you've probably been sending out signals that any normal male could pick up. So this guy must be either dumb, blind, incredibly stupid, or all three. Get him to take you to his place, build a fire, put on some music, and hand the jerk a bottle of wine. But if you have to go to all that trouble, you'll probably be very disappointed when he finally does get around to making a pass."

Toni was sure that it wasn't her imagination. Kyle had actually sounded jealous.

Her elbow was resting on the arm of the chair, and she put her hand to her forehead. Turning her smile to the wall, she prayed that the giggle in her throat wouldn't escape.

Kyle was neither dumb nor blind. Incredibly stupid was up for grabs. There was already a fire in the fireplace. A soothing ballad played softly on the stereo, blending with the melody of the rain. The remnants of the wine they'd had with dinner filled their glasses, the empty bottle now sitting on the coffee table. And Kyle was seriously underestimating his lovemaking, though he quite obviously didn't know that it was his own prowess he'd just criticized.

He certainly wasn't being very cooperative in planning his seduction though.

"Thanks, Kyle," she mumbled, suppressing her grin as she opened her file again. "You've been an enormous help."

When she picked up her things to go to bed twenty minutes later, Kyle was still buried under the newspaper. As she walked past his reclining form and said good-night, she dropped the empty wine bottle on his stomach.

A weak September sun tried vainly to shine the next morning. Madeline had assured Toni that a little rain wouldn't prevent Kyle and "the boys" from playing their usual Saturday football

game. Kyle had mentioned the game last weekend, and Toni had every intention of going
today.

The quiet discussion taking place between the
two women now had nothing to do with either
the game or the weather. Taking advantage of
the easy friendship developing between her and
Madeline, Toni had asked her the same questions she had put to Kyle last night. No names
were mentioned, of course. And if Madeline
suspected anything, she was kind enough to
keep it to herself.

"You just leave it to me," Madeline said, patting the sleeve of Toni's bulky white pullover.
"I've got just what you need. Since I don't live
too far from here, I'll run by my apartment after
I pick up Kyle's cleaning." The sound of heavy
footsteps approaching the kitchen caused her
voice to drop to a whisper as she quickly added,
"I'll put the box in your closet."

The box? The pale brown arches of Toni's
eyebrows snapped together as she opened her
mouth to ask Madeline what she was talking
about, but the deep resonance of Kyle's voice cut
her off.

"They turn the heat off in your office?"

Toni dismissed the odd flutter of her pulse,
telling herself that it was ridiculous to be affected by the sound of someone's voice. The
questioning frown that had been meant for Madeline was redirected to Kyle. What was *he* talking about?

She didn't have to ask. Her expression did it
for her.

"The way you're dressed," he prompted,

sounding as if those ambiguous words should clarify everything.

Crossing his arms over the very faded "10" on the old football jersey he was wearing, his dark eyes slid over her heavy, cabled sweater, down the line of her rather snug corduroy pants and settled on her calfskin boots.

When his deceptively disinterested gaze finally returned to the knot of silken hair on her head, she realized what he was talking about. She probably would have understood sooner if her senses hadn't developed the maddening habit of short-circuiting every time she saw him.

"I'm not going to the office right now." With more boldness than she was feeling at the moment, she returned his appraisal with one of her own. How could a pair of washed-out jeans with torn knees look so terrific? "I thought I'd been invited to a football game."

"You mean you're actually going to take a weekend off?"

"Cute, Donovan," she chided, returning his teasing smile with mock exasperation. "I'll go in tomorrow. But I could hardly pass up a chance like this. It might be kind of interesting watching them pull you out of the mud. And"—she nodded toward the window—"from the way it was raining last night and the looks of the sky right now, there should be plenty of it in the park."

Kyle's eyes were still on Toni, but his words were directed to the woman with the silly smile plastered on her pleasant face. "She talks bravely, Madeline."

Madeline didn't acknowledge Kyle's remark.

She just mumbled a barely audible, "See you two later," and started humming to herself as she headed downstairs to fold the laundry.

Toni could have shot her. The tune she was humming was the "Wedding March."

Apparently Kyle didn't notice. With a gallant sweep of his hand, he gestured for Toni to precede him out of the kitchen. "You know," he said as she started past him, "it might be kind of interesting seeing you covered with mud, too, Collins."

"I can't imagine how that would happen," she returned smugly, her mind racing with the possibilities of how he could accomplish that feat. She could think of worse things than being tackled by Kyle. "I'm not playing. I'm only going to watch."

There was something in his deep chuckle that sounded like a provocative warning. "Oh, you don't have to play." His hand settled on her back as he nudged her toward the front door. It was a simple gesture. Completely platonic. But that didn't stop the crazy tremors from racing through her stomach and down her legs. "There are other ways for a person to get a little muddy. And I really should get even with you for nailing me with that wine bottle last night. What did you do that for anyway?"

Toni barely glanced up as she accompanied him down the front steps to the car. "Just seemed like the thing to do." She shrugged, thinking how right he was about the "guy" being dense. Maybe she should have hit him over the head with it.

It could have been a product of wishful thinking, but Toni was almost positive that there was some subtle difference in Kyle's attitude toward her. She was more convinced than ever when they reached the park and his teasing, brotherly manner fell away for a few very revealing moments.

Several of the men Kyle played football with were already out in the middle of the soggy field, and two of them broke away when they saw Kyle's Porsche pull into the tree-lined parking lot.

"Toni Collins!" Todd Ruger came lumbering forward and wrapped her in a bone-crushing hug before she'd even closed the car door. "I couldn't believe it when Kyle said you were back. And working for the competition! You look great, kid. Just great!"

"Thanks, Todd," Toni laughed, leaving her arms around his waist. She tipped her head back to see if five years had made any difference in his little-boy face. They hadn't. Todd still looked as cute as ever—if a six-foot-three-inch, two-hundred-pound-plus bear could be called cute. "You don't look so bad yourself. How's Trista and the kids?"

Todd's grin faltered briefly. "Trista and I split a couple of years ago. But I've got the boys this weekend." He jerked his head toward the two towheaded eight-year-old twins chasing a soccer ball. "You really look great," he repeated. "Doesn't she, Jerry?"

Toni wanted to tell Todd that she was sorry about him and his wife, but she didn't get the chance. Jerry Andrews, a man of considerably less bulk than the one still holding her loosely, stepped beside her. He wasn't anywhere near as effusive as Todd, but his greeting was just as genuine.

Jerry and Todd were both talking, almost simultaneously, and Toni was trying to keep up with their questions when she glanced over at Kyle.

Her spirits, already in pretty good shape, soared.

Kyle's jaw was clenched so tightly that she thought his teeth might shatter. Though his arms were crossed, she could see his hands balling into tight fists and the muscles in his neck flexing tautly. It was hard to tell which looked more ominous—the gray clouds boiling overhead, or Kyle's gray-black eyes.

Odd things to feel elated about, but it was what was causing him to look so wonderfully dangerous that filled Toni with a heady exhilaration.

He was glaring at Todd's hand, now resting lightly around her shoulders, and at her arm, still slung around Todd's waist.

It took every ounce of control Toni had to keep her face from registering acknowledgment of what she was seeing in Kyle's eyes. There was a fierce possession revealed in those glittering depths, and the unmistakable signs of a man struggling to restrain himself.

Within seconds that forbidding expression vanished, to be replaced with a tight, but affable, smile.

"Come on you guys," he muttered goodnaturedly. "You can stand around and rehash old war stories later." His hand grasped Toni's elbow a little too firmly, and he pulled her away from Todd. "We've got a game to play."

Kyle had recovered so quickly that neither Jerry nor Todd had noticed his momentarily challenging stance. But Toni had. And that was all that mattered. She didn't even notice how cold the wind was that ruffled Kyle's hair as she sank down onto the long wooden bench and watched the three men jog out onto the field.

With the exception of Todd's boys, the other men's families had elected to stay home where it was warm and dry. Toni didn't feel the need for company right then anyway. The thoughts that warmed her against the cold mist now dampening her sweater and clinging in jewellike clusters to her hair were company enough.

How was she ever going to get him to kiss her again?

Her eyes, like her thoughts, were on Kyle. He was running with his head tucked low and his broad shoulders hunched forward. She saw his arms shoot out just as the hulk with the football wedged against his stomach tried to dodge him, and both the hulk and the ball hit the ground with a thud.

Nice tackle, she smiled to herself, and immediately returned to her contemplation.

She thought about just initiating a kiss herself, but summarily dismissed that idea. Her aggressiveness didn't extend to that kind of behavior. Calling the shots at work was one thing; this was another matter entirely. Somehow she'd have to maneuver it so Kyle would take the initiative. How was she going to do that? A thoughtful frown knitted her brow.

Maybe whatever was in Madeline's "box" would help.

She was trying to figure out what could be in that box—discarding the more ridiculous possibilities like black lace garters and love potions—when she saw Kyle lunge for the ball, and three men pile on top of him.

Arms, legs and torsos emerged from the lopsided human pyramid, and the three men struggled to their feet. Kyle didn't.

Visions of him lying there unconscious skittered through her brain, and within seconds she was off the bench and running toward the field. She could almost see him lying there broken and . . .

Immediately she checked herself, grateful that she was still a good distance away. Kyle was up and being led to his car, supported by two men she had been introduced to an hour earlier as Les and Gary. Kyle's jersey, as well as his jeans and the side of his face, were covered with mud. And he was holding his side. She wasn't sure, but it sounded like he was laughing.

Making a deliberate effort to hide the initial fear that had sent her vaulting like a frantic mother bear rescuing her cub, she crossed her arms in a gesture of calm complacence and headed for the car, too. He'd scared the living daylights out of her, and she'd almost succeeded in making a total fool of herself. She could just imagine the other men's reactions—not to mention Kyle's—if she'd raced out there and blurted out something nice and simple like *Don't die, Kyle! I love you!*

It was disgust at her overreaction—this business of being in love definitely altered common sense—that made her hug her arms defensively as she approached the group now standing by Kyle's Porsche.

"You big idiot," she mumbled, hoping her more protective emotions were masked from the others as she rapidly scanned Kyle's face. He was grinning! "Don't you think that was a rather unintelligent thing to do?"

Drying his face with the towel Gary had handed him, he tossed her an indifferent glance, then flipped the towel onto the hood. "What do you know about football?" He winced, hugging his side again, then tried to look casual as he leaned against the fender.

"Very little," she admitted honestly, wondering why men always had to put on such a brave front. "But I know enough not to jump on a ball when there's three guys the size of Mack trucks running at me."

Two of those guys, Les and Gary, looked at her sheepishly. It was Les who spoke. "I think we just knocked the wind out of him." Drawing his hand through his tangled brown hair, he turned back to Kyle. "I think that's all we did anyway. Sure hope you didn't break a rib or something."

"It'd take more than you featherweights to do any serious damage," Kyle quipped with typical male equanimity. A stoic smile creased his attractive and mud-streaked features.

One of Todd's boys came racing up, his soccer ball tucked under his arm. "Boy! That was neat!" His chubby little face was bright with wide-eyed admiration. "My dad really nailed ya, didn't he?"

"Yeah," Kyle groaned, still managing to look undaunted as he ruffled the child's hair. "He sure did, Davie."

Toni didn't miss the obvious affection Kyle had for the child who was now asking if he was all right. But the instant he glanced over at her and saw the soft light in her eyes, he turned his attention to the men, all but ignoring Davie.

Toni was a little puzzled at the obviousness of his action. For someone whose attitude had always included an intense dislike of children, there had been an awful lot of warmth in that brief exchange—as much warmth as there was coolness in his quickly shuttered expression when he'd caught her watching him. She didn't quite know what to make of that and, with a mental shrug, turned her attention back to the men.

Apparently it was an unspoken rule that when one of their friends got hurt, that was the end of the game. Within seconds, a half-dozen other men—all looking just as wet and dirty as Kyle—descended on them. Toni edged around to the other side of the car.

Being the only female present, she suddenly felt a little out of place in the midst of the ensuing male camaraderie. Concern for Kyle was evident by the back-slapping and free-flowing advice—which ranged from everything to going to get an x-ray to anesthetizing the pain with Scotch—and Toni had the feeling that any feminine concern would be an unwelcomed intrusion. Kyle didn't look like he needed her anyway.

That hurt.

It was several minutes before the crowd dispersed and the men headed to their own cars. Toni had taken a clean towel from Kyle's sports bag and handed it to him.

"Are you all right?" she asked, watching his face disappear behind the striped terrycloth.

His response was muffled, but distinctly defensive. "I'm fine."

Toni's jaw tightened. "The guys are gone, Kyle," she stated tersely, turning to open the car door. "So you can drop the macho act. If you're hurt, tell me. And give me your keys."

"I said, I'm fine. And I'll drive."

Toni raised her eyes heavenward and blinked back the raindrops that landed on her face. "Don't be ridiculous, Donovan. You *are* hurt and I'm perfectly capable of driving. Now, can you get in the car by yourself? Or do you plan on riding home on the fender?"

Kyle frowned at the edge in her voice and pushed himself away from the car. It was apparent enough that he was just as puzzled by her tone as she was.

Toni had no idea why she was acting like this. She was so afraid that Kyle might really be injured, yet something was preventing her from showing that worry. So what if he'd ignored her a few minutes ago? It was stupid to be miffed because she'd been excluded from the convivial group of men.

The irony of the situation struck her as she

watched Kyle carefully lower himself into the passenger seat. He had reacted in much the same way when she'd been talking with Todd and Jerry when they'd first arrived at the park. Was her behavior as revealing as his had been?

She slid behind the wheel and, after starting the engine, turned on the heater. Her eyes were still on the temperature switch when she quietly said, "Take off your shirt."

Kyle's eyes darted to her. "What?"

"You heard me." Her lips curved mischievously as she pushed a damp strand of hair from her face. If it hadn't been for the fact that Kyle was in pain, the situation could have presented some interesting possibilities. "It's soaking wet and"—she motioned to where his muddy sleeve had brushed against the seat—"you're getting the car dirty. Besides, I can't see what you did to yourself unless you . . ."

"I didn't do anything to myself," he interrupted, staring down at the hole in the knee of his jeans.

"Then why haven't you let go of your side?"

"Because I'm cold?" he ventured.

"All the more reason to take off that wet shirt."

He clearly didn't want to comply. "Well, if you won't buy that excuse, how about . . ."

It occurred to her then that maybe he *couldn't* take it off. "Can you lift your arms?" she cut in.

The slight tightening of his jaw told her nothing.

For a moment, Toni had been entertaining the idea of using this opportunity to provoke some kind of response from him. But the dullness in his eyes and the way he seemed to wince whenever he moved told her that now was not the time to play temptress.

His jersey was partially loosened from the waistband of his jeans. Telling herself that the only reason she was doing this was to see how badly he was hurt—maybe he did need an x-ray —she reached over and lifted his hand from where he was clutching his left side.

The instant her warm hand folded over his cooler one, she felt him stiffen. He said nothing though, and with her heart beating in her throat, she pulled his shirt free of his pants and started to lift up the soggy fabric.

"Gee, Collins," Kyle said, trying to chuckle but apparently deciding that it wasn't worth the effort, or the pain, "I didn't know you cared."

"Well, I do." Could he hear any deeper meaning in her voice? "So, help me peel this thing off, will you? Lift your arm."

He did, slowly testing the motion to see how much pain was going to be involved, then managed a relieved smile when it didn't cause too much additional discomfort.

The material clung damply, and as Toni pushed it up she could see a faint, but distinctly football-shaped, patch of red covering his ribs.

Instinct drew her fingers to that sore-looking outline, and she gently traced over it. She tried not to think about how good it felt to touch him, or how badly she wanted to run her fingers through the dark hairs curling over his broad chest. His muscles grew rigid beneath her hand,

and she saw his chest expand with his quick, quietly drawn breath. A fine blanket of goose bumps sprang up on his skin.

His voice sounded husky. "I think you're right about getting out of this thing. Get my jacket, will you? It's behind the seat."

Reluctantly Toni pulled back and, pulling herself to her knees, reached between the seats. She heard a hiss of air being drawn through his teeth and felt, rather than saw, him leaning toward the dashboard.

"Hold it a minute," she sighed, bumping his shoulder and streaking mud down the front of her sweater as she settled back on her side. Sportscars were so blasted small! "What are you trying to do?"

"I'm *trying* to turn on the defroster."

It had begun raining in earnest now. Cold, fat drops pelted the roof, and the warmth of their breath had fogged up the windows.

Toni flipped the lever he'd been trying to reach and dropped his jacket between them. She grasped the edge of his sleeve. "Pull your arm out."

Between the two of them they managed to get the jersey off—a fair amount of mud now clinging to Toni—and she started to zip him into his running jacket. Though he kept insisting that nothing was broken, he finally did admit to being a little sore.

He had been muttering something about not being totally helpless—a clearly debatable issue at the moment—when she raised her eyes to meet the smile in his.

She was draped over the console, and his hand

was resting by her hip. His head was only inches away, and as she saw that smile fading, her fingers stilled in the middle of his chest.

Suddenly, it seemed very quiet. And that silence seemed to take on the same intensity she was now seeing in his smoldering gray eyes. Toni's heart felt it had just stopped, then jerked back to life in frantic double-time.

Kyle's gaze slowly caressed her face, becoming more heated as it lingered on her softly parted mouth. She felt his hand brush against her corduroy-covered thigh.

All she would have to do is lean forward a little and . . .

"Toni," Kyle whispered thickly, his breath fanning her cheek. "I need . . ."

His hand, still lying lightly against her thigh, pressed more firmly. It felt like he had just made a fist.

"What do you need, Kyle?" Her voice was quiet, and heavy with anticipation.

The desire so evident in his eyes disappeared abruptly, and he put his other hand on her shoulder, nudging her down to her seat. "I need a shower," he muttered, scowling down at the mud drying on his jeans. Running his index finger across his knee, he glanced sideways at Toni, then turned to run his finger down her nose. She caught a glimpse of his familiar, teasing grin.

Slanting him a peevish glance—one that could have been interpreted as either disappointment at what hadn't happened, or annoyance at what he'd just done—she started to wipe the mud from her nose.

"Leave it," he chuckled, grabbing her wrist and placing her hand on the wheel. "There's something about seeing a princess with a little dirt on her face that's sort of appealing."

Her mouth twisted wryly as she wiped the mud off anyway. "You have a very perverted sense of . . ."

"Beauty?" he offered.

No, she corrected mentally, backing the car out of the parking space. *Timing!*

They were half way home before Kyle convinced Toni that he didn't need to see a doctor, and the subject of his bruised ribs was abandoned. "Do you have a date with Greg tonight?" Kyle asked with credible casualness.

The rain demanded that she pay attention to the wet streets, so she couldn't do much more than glance at him. He was looking out his window. "I don't have any plans for the evening. Why?"

"Just curious. When do you plan on starting the great seduction?"

Somehow his last two words sounded like they should begin with capital letters.

"What makes you think it's Greg I'm . . . ah . . . interested in?"

"You mean you're seeing someone else, too?"

The car behind them pulled out to pass, so Toni could only imagine Kyle's apoplectic expression. "Yes, I am. I see him quite a bit actually. And since you brought it up, maybe you could help me. . . ."

"Listen," he interjected quickly. "I've got to be in Portland the first part of next week, so would you mind checking with Madeline when

she comes in on Wednesday to make sure everything'll be ready for next Saturday night? I won't
be getting home until late Friday and . . ."

Kyle wasn't acting like Kyle at all. Never had
he refused to discuss a subject with her, and his
abrupt turn in the conversation was glaringly
obvious.

It was also apparent that he didn't know that
he was the subject that had just been dropped so
quickly.

". . . So you won't mind taking care of things
for me?" he concluded when she pulled the car
into the drive.

Toni cut the engine and turned deceivingly
cool blue eyes to him. She'd always been quite
good at hiding her feelings, but she had the
feeling that her mask had developed a few
cracks. She didn't want to hide anything from
Kyle now anyway. "Don't worry about the
party," she smiled. "I'm sure Madeline's got
everything under control. Now, stay put for a
minute and I'll help you out."

Surprisingly enough, Kyle didn't argue. And
when he eased himself out of the car and she
slid her arm around his waist, she could have
sworn that his lips brushed the top of her head.
His right arm was draped over her shoulder, but
when she glanced up there was nothing in his
expression to indicate that anything of the sort
had happened at all. Did she want him so much
that she was beginning to imagine things? Just
as she was imagining that his fingers were
lightly caressing her arm as they ascended the
stairs and stopped in front of the door?

"Your hair's wet," Kyle scolded, patting her on

the head as if she were a child. "And you must be freezing. Your sweater's damp, too." He made a tsking sound with his tongue. "Not to mention dirty."

The teasing affection in his voice sounded more brotherly than anything else, and her more wild imaginings rapidly vanished.

"I'm not cold," she retorted, sliding her key into the lock.

His arm was still supporting part of his weight by resting on her shoulder. The warmth of his body permeated her sweater and the side of her pants where his hip pressed against her.

He drew her closer. "If you're not cold, then how come you're shivering?"

Another shudder ran through her. It had nothing to do with temperature extremes. External ones, anyway.

When she didn't respond, or make any attempt to move, Kyle pushed the door open with his foot. "Come on, princess. I know what you need to warm you up."

Toni told herself not to get her hopes up, but she couldn't deny the tiny thrill of excitement racing through her when his arm tightened and he guided her into the entryway. She was so caught up in that sudden rush of expectancy that she didn't even notice how easily Kyle was moving.

At least she didn't notice it until he walked over to the wet bar in the living room and reached for a bottle of brandy.

"Here," he said, handing her a snifter of deep amber liquid. "This should help. A hot shower probably wouldn't hurt either." Anticipation sank to deflation as he tapped the end of her nose. "You did get a little muddy, you know?"

His hand was clutching his side again as he headed down the hall to his room.

Toni, with a slightly frustrated shrug, took a sip of the brandy and headed straight for her closet.

Chapter Five

*K*yle peeled his clothes off and dropped them on the black tiles of his bathroom floor. Glancing at his naked reflection in the mirror, he tentatively felt the oval bruise on his ribs. When he touched it, it just hurt. But when Toni's fingers had so gently traced over his skin, he hadn't even been aware of the pain. Just like he'd forgotten about it when she'd helped him into the house. He hadn't needed her assistance. But it was such a perfect excuse to feel her against him again that he couldn't pass it up.

Turning the shower on full blast, he stepped under the steamy spray. Toni had been right. The combined weight of Les, Todd and Gary *had* felt like a Mack truck. With a groan, he reached for the shampoo and dumped a liberal amount on his head—thinking that, right after he washed it, he should probably have it examined.

He had come so close to repeating the same mistake he'd made the other night. While Toni had been helping him out of his jersey and into his jacket, all he could think about was how wonderful it would feel to bury his hands in her hair and draw that gorgeous mouth to his. It had taken a moment for the message in her darkening eyes to register, but when it had, thankfully, he'd regained his senses. She had been concerned about him. That was all. And it was only the type of concern one friend feels for another. He'd noticed her acting a little strangely lately—wary maybe?—but he was sure that it was only because she didn't want to risk a repeat of his performance the other night. She was so clearly going out of her way *not* to mention it. And she was making it very evident that she was interested in someone else.

Toni pulled open her closet doors and looked down at the floor. There, just as Madeline had promised, was a box. She could hear Kyle's shower running across the hall, and deciding that her own shower could wait, she knelt down and pulled the box toward her.

Her eyebrows knitted together as she lifted the lid and picked up the note lying on top of the books.

I picked out the ones that I thought would be most helpful, and by the time you finish reading these, I'm sure you'll have come up with a plan that's guaranteed to sabotage his defenses. Let me know if you need more. Good luck with your research, and with him. Love, Madeline.

P.S. Don't worry, I won't breathe a word.

"You won't have to, Madeline." Toni smiled, picking up one of the books. "Not if you waltz around here humming the 'Wedding March.'"

Flipping through the pages, Toni drew in a deep breath and pushed the carton to the back of her closet. She'd get started on her "research" right after she got cleaned up. It was a good thing she was a fast reader. There had to be at least three dozen romance novels in that box!

Three hours later, Toni lay sprawled across her bed. After a quick shower, she'd pulled on a pair of soft chamois slacks and a huge raglan-sleeve sweater. Her hair floated across her back in a gossamer veil, and shoving back the long tresses that kept falling over her shoulder, she propped herself up on her elbow and turned another page.

Her mind was already analyzing some of the scenes she'd read, paring them down to fit into the plan that was already formulating. Seducing Kyle looked like it might be fun—if she could just get up her nerve.

Nerves seemed to be in abundant supply at the moment. Thinking about Kyle in some of those scenes was playing absolute havoc with her nervous system. Whew! she thought, with an audible sigh. The hero certainly fits Kyle's description. But I'm lacking in a few pertinent areas.

Toni wasn't going to dwell on insignificant

details at the moment. The overall picture was
what was important. The erotic scene she'd just
read had taken place on a bearskin rug in front
of a roaring fire. The heroine had been drenched
to the skin after falling into an ice-encrusted
lake, and the hero had taken her into his cabin to
warm her.

With an ironic chuckle, Toni closed the book
and propped her chin on her crossed arms. When
she and Kyle had gotten home, she'd been cold—
nothing like the woman in the book, but definitely chilly. If she'd been on her toes, she might
have maneuvered Kyle into the living room
where they could have built a fire and . . . "He
would have handed me a glass of brandy and
disappeared," she mumbled, completing her
thought.

Angled as she was across her bed, she could
see her door being opened slightly and Kyle's
frame shadowing the two-inch space. Just as
she jerked her head up, the door swung wide and
Kyle leaned against the doorjamb. His shirt was
unbuttoned, revealing a good portion of the
chest she'd envisioned in the mythical firelight.
Her throat felt very, very dry.

"I would have knocked, but I didn't want to
disturb you. Just wanted to see if you were
asleep."

"I was reading." Somehow she forced her eyes
away from where they'd wandered to the swirl of
dark hair above the waistband of his cords. "You
look like you just woke up."

Kyle watched as she swung her legs around to
sit on the edge of the bed. "I did. And you look

about sixteen years old with your hair down like that."

"I know." Gathering a handful of hair between her fingers and thumb, she began twisting it into a coil. "That's why I wear it up. Image, you know."

"I like it down. You hungry?"

His comment was made quite absently, but Toni let her hair fall back down around her shoulders. "A little. Did you want me to fix lunch?"

A lazy smile creased his sleepy features. "Since it's almost five-thirty, I think dinner might be more appropriate. But it's my turn to cook, and since that's the last thing I feel like doing, I'll just go get us some hamburgers. Want one?"

Toni's eyes shifted back to his open shirt. Though the fabric covered most of it, she could see the edge of a very angry looking bruise. "How are you feeling?"

"Stiff."

"I'm not surprised. And you're in no shape to go anywhere." Lifting herself from the bed, she pulled the hem of her sweater over her hips and started toward the door. "I'll fix dinner."

Kyle must have still been groggy from his nap. There was an unfamiliar vulnerability in his expression, and Toni was certain that he didn't even know it was there.

"You're an angel," he sighed when she stepped in front of him to turn out the light.

Her heart raced like a triphammer as she reached up to push away the lock of hair that lay over his forehead. "Thanks, Kyle." She smiled, gratified by the way his whole body had just seemed to tense—and adding to herself that he probably wouldn't think she was much of an angel if he knew what she was up to.

The second she had touched him, that vulnerability had vanished. As she walked away, she could feel his cool, questioning eyes on her back. *Plan I: The Subtle Approach* had just been put into action.

Even the most well thought-out plans develop a few snags.

If Kyle noticed that Toni was using every imaginable excuse to touch him, he was doing a remarkable job of hiding it. She placed her hand on his shoulder to lean from behind him and set his plate on the table. Twice, she curled her fingers around his forearm while they were talking. She let her hand rest on his hip when he pulled his shirt back to show her the darkening bruise and touched it gently.

The only reaction she got was the slight stiffening of his muscles—and a comment that her hands were cold.

She told herself not to be discouraged. Though he was doing nothing to take advantage of her lead, he wasn't doing anything to dissuade her either. As they sat in the living room watching television from opposite ends of the sofa, she was achingly aware of the way his eyes would fall to her mouth when she spoke, and especially with the fascination he had with her hair as she absently sifted the long strands through her fingers. Was he remembering how it had felt in his own fingers? The darkness in his eyes told her that he was.

Toni was quietly pleased with what she appeared to be accomplishing. He couldn't seem to keep his eyes off of her, and that was enough for now. He really wasn't in any condition to succumb to more flagrant inducements anyway. He wasn't moving with his usual ease, and the pinched line of his mouth told her that any moaning he'd be doing would hardly be groans of ecstasy. His side was hurting, even though he kept insisting that it didn't.

Tonight, she'd just have to settle for an evening with him in front of the TV. That wasn't so bad. Loving someone meant sharing the quiet times, too. In many ways, she found that very satisfying.

It would have been a lot more satisfying if his arm had been around her, though.

Sunday afternoon held no promise of further accomplishments.

Toni was curled up in the chair by the window reading one of Madeline's books from behind a copy of *Forbes* while Kyle sat on the sofa watching a football game. No doubt he was silently identifying with the linebacker whose progress had just been abruptly halted by the massive shoulder that connected with his stomach. Though Kyle hadn't been complaining about it, Toni could tell from the way he kept rubbing the back of his neck that he'd hurt more than his side when he'd been tackled.

Every time he flinched, Toni's heart gave a

funny little jerk, and she longed to do something —anything—to ease his discomfort. He'd been growling like a wounded bear all day, and she was sure that he was irritated with the inconvenience of his injury as much as anything else.

Closing her book on the provocative massage sequence she'd been reading—she decided that the massage was in order, even if the more boldly explicit moves portrayed in the chapter were not. Right now anyway.

"Your neck hurt?" she asked, climbing onto the sofa beside him.

His eyes were on the television, and his hand still gripped the back of his neck. "It's fine."

Ignoring his terse disclaimer with a rueful shake of her head, she scooted back on the sofa and tucked her legs beneath her. He was just being obstinate, and having been blessed with her fair share of that same trait, she pushed his hand away and settled hers in its place.

His muscles turned to stone, and he jerked around sideways to face her, immediately clamping his hand over the strained muscles again. "Aw, damn." He grimaced at the pain slicing down his shoulder. He shouldn't have moved so quickly. "What are you trying to do?"

Calm blue eyes blinked at his narrow-eyed expression. "I'm returning a favor. Now move back here."

"What favor?"

"Do you remember the morning you massaged my legs because they were so sore? Well," she continued, letting the shadow of wariness in his eyes answer her question, "you look like you could use a little of that same medicine. And stop looking at me like that. It's not like I'm trying to seduce you or something."

Her last words were directed to the pulse beating at the base of his neck. There was no way she could have said that if she'd been looking him straight in the eye—even though there was a certain amount of truth to her statement at the moment.

"It only hurts a little," he qualified, allowing Toni to position herself behind him.

Toni raised her eyes to the ceiling, begging the deities above to enlighten her as to why he hated to admit that he wasn't invincible. But she didn't need Zeus to hit her with a lightning bolt to know that Kyle was just being Kyle.

She reached for his shoulders.

Her knees were wedged around his hips and as her fingers worked slowly over the pale green fabric of his shirt, she didn't know who this exercise was affecting more. A massage was supposed to relax a person. But the muscles where her hands deftly pressed along his spine were positively rigid; and the one spanning her stomach felt like it had just balled up into a quivering knot.

"Toni?" Kyle began, his head lolling forward when her fingers sank into the crisp hairs at his nape again, "you didn't stay home from work today because of me, did you?"

Her hands splayed over his back, her palms making deep circles. If she pushed hard, he wouldn't be able to feel the betraying tremors in her fingers. "I stayed home because it's Sunday," she replied, negating what she'd said yesterday about going into the office today. She'd have to stay late every night this week to play catch-up. "I've been thinking about what you said about taking time off to relax, and decided that now's as good as any time to start." She really hadn't thought about it until now. She wasn't about to let her job suffer, but she wanted to spend as much time as she could with Kyle. Soon enough, she'd have to start looking for a place of her own. In the meantime, she wanted to let him know that she cared—subtly, of course. "Even if it hadn't been the weekend," she continued, trailing her fingertips down his back, "I would have stayed home if you needed me."

Kyle said nothing, his only sound a tiny moan as she reversed her motion and dipped her fingers beneath his collar. The muscles there were considerably more supple, and she felt him shudder.

"I guess I owe you a turn at KP," he mumbled, evading her remarks. "Thanks for cooking dinner last night."

Her tone was light and mildly teasing. Every time she lightened the pressure of her hands, she could feel him tense a little more, and she had the feeling that he was trying not to think about what she was doing. "Oh, I plan on getting even with you. You can take me out to some fabulously expensive restaurant and I'll have . . ."

"You can have anything you want," he interrupted with a sigh.

"Anything?"

"You name it. Whatever . . . mmm . . . that feels good."

Repeating the motion that had elicited his sigh, she tried to keep her tone as conversational as she could. No mean feat, considering what she was doing now. "We'll discuss what I want when you feel better," she said, pulling his shirttail free from his jeans.

Sliding her hands up under his shirt, she swallowed hard and fought the desire simply to close her eyes and relish the feel of his smooth skin. If she closed her eyes, she would be able to see all too clearly the scene she had just finished reading a while ago. Though there was no warm, scented oil easing the friction between her hands and Kyle's back, and his fingers weren't tracing tantalizing paths over her arms and across her breasts, she could . . .

Knock it off, Toni! she chastised herself, and shoved his shirt up to the middle of his back with more abruptness than was necessary. It was taking a supreme amount of effort to remind herself that this was *not* part of the Great Seduction. At least, it hadn't started out that way.

Tucking her bottom lip between her teeth, she hastily reevaluated the situation. Kyle's neck didn't seem to be bothering him anywhere near as much as it had been. His breathing did seem a little irregular though. And he kept leaning against her hands to deepen their pressure when she massaged the small of his back.

It looked like it was time to abandon the more altruistic aspects of this massage.

Hoping that he couldn't hear the deeper huskiness in her voice, she slowly lowered his shirt. "This would be a lot easier to do if you'd take this off, Kyle."

The moan that escaped from his throat was barely audible. The thick sound was definitely not one of pain, and she felt a curious sense of feminine power encouraging more daring behavior.

Raising herself up on her knees, she pressed herself against his back and reached around his neck to unbutton his shirt herself. Her face brushed the roughness of his cheek, and she could smell the spicy clean scent of his aftershave. Though she was the only one moving, she couldn't tell who was being seduced by whom at the moment.

A strangled gasp was compressed between Kyle's lips as Toni loosened the buttons from their holes and drew his shirt away to continue her agonizing massage. He was convinced that she didn't know what she was doing to him, how sensual her caresses were. She was simply returning a favor. To a friend, he reminded himself forcefully, nearly dying when her hands slid over his shoulders and sank into the dark hairs on his chest. The woman was a witch. An absolute sorceress. Her hands could turn cold stone into warm clay. And he felt about as malleable as that now.

Telling himself that he was only imagining the erotic undertones in Toni's touch because he wanted her so badly, he groped for something to talk about. Anything to get his mind off of what she was doing. Anything except her boyfriends. He couldn't quite stomach those conversations. He decided to ask about her mother.

Toni had told him long ago that her father had died when she was six, leaving her mother quite well off. Caroline Collins's global jaunts seemed like a safe topic.

For a second, it felt like Toni's hands went limp at the subject he had just proposed. But Kyle thought that it was just because he had moved a little too suggestively when her fingers had touched the sensitive nerve at the base of his spine. He willed himself to be perfectly still when her palms planted themselves firmly in the middle of his back.

Her breath feathered the hairs on the back of his head while she told him about her mother's recent trip to France. Kyle tried to pay attention, but no mortal male could concentrate on the quaint little villages in Bordeaux's wine district when a husky-voiced woman who smelled like powder and gardenias was practically breathing in his ear.

Toni's face was actually a good foot away from his ear, but Kyle wasn't terribly aware of major details at the moment. Her hands had just wandered down and were pressing into the skin just above the waistband of his jeans again. She was courting disaster by rubbing him there.

He knew that the seams of his pants came with a life-time guarantee against stress. Wryly he wondered if that same guarantee applied to the zipper.

Barely glancing behind him, he grasped her

wrist and pushed her hand upward. "Rub my neck a little more," he said, hating the thickness in his voice.

That wasn't really where he wanted her hand. But he could only imagine what she would do if he put it where he did want it. One set of bruised ribs was enough.

The slight tightening of her thighs around his hips when she moved forward resulted in his slowly exhaled breath. Images he knew he was better off not thinking about flashed vividly in his mind.

Don't you think you'd be more comfortable if you lay down?" Practicality had prompted Toni's suggestion. She didn't want to stop—it was heaven to be able to touch him—but her legs were getting cramped and she needed to switch positions. He didn't look too comfortable perched like a statue on the edge of the sofa anyway.

Lying down was the last thing Kyle wanted to do. It was taking every bit of control he had not to turn around and press her into the cushions, taste the sweet warmth of her mouth that he remembered so well. A man could only push himself so far. And Kyle had just reached his limit.

"Your hands are probably getting tired," he hedged, picking his shirt up from the floor and pulling himself to his feet.

A million tiny needles jabbed into her legs as she untangled them and glanced up at Kyle's slightly flushed features. She had the feeling that her color was heightened, too. The feel of his body still burned on her hands.

Kyle refused to look at her and skirted the sofa to start down the hall. "Thanks for the back rub," he added flatly. "I think I'll go take a hot shower to finish what you started. That should get the rest of the kinks out."

The shower he was going to take definitely wasn't going to be a hot one. Once safely inside his room, he scattered socks, jeans and jockey shorts in a winding path to his bathroom. "If cleanliness is next to godliness," he muttered, bracing himself against the icy spray, "then I'm destined for sainthood."

Toni leaned against the back of the sofa and stared at the glass figurine on the coffee table. As a seductress, she was an absolute flop. Kyle was physically attracted to her. Feminine instinct told her that much. But why was he holding back?

Flipping her hair over her shoulder, she rubbed her numb legs. There was more than a physical attraction between them. His affection was far too apparent for her to think otherwise. Did he realize that they knew each other so well, it would be impossible to separate feelings from any physical display of caring? Had he been hurt so badly by his ex-wife that he simply couldn't handle an emotional relationship?

Toni knew from their conversations in the past that his relationships with women involved little more than sex. *Their* relationship, for all practical purposes, included everything *but* that. Why couldn't he bring the two together?

She could think of only one reason that might answer her exasperated questions. Kyle was probably so used to thinking of her as a sort of little sister that he couldn't think of her as a woman. She didn't want to buy that logic though. He had responded to her—once.

And she wanted him to do it again. She was tired of having to restrain herself when she wanted to put her arms around him. She wanted to be able to touch him without pretext. Soothe the tiredness from him when he came home looking absolutely beat after an especially trying day—not just hand him a glass of wine and ask him to tell her about it. Verbal communication was important. But she wanted to touch him without feeling like she was treading on forbidden ground.

"Damn it, Donovan," she swore, jerking herself to her feet. "I'm *not* your sister! I'm a woman, and I love you."

History has long since proven that a woman in love is not the most rational creature in the world.

Kyle was leaving for Portland in the morning. But when he got back, *Plan II: The Not-So-Subtle Approach* was going into effect. Toni had no idea what that plan was, but by the time she finished a few more of Madeline's books, she'd think of something. Kyle had always maintained that nothing was ever handed to a person on a silver platter. If you wanted something, you had to work for it, and you should never let anyone or anything stand in your way if you think it is worth having.

Well, Kyle Donovan—stubborn and thick-headed as he was—was certainly worth having.

She'd waited all of her life for Kyle. And whatever portion he wanted of the rest of it was his for the asking.

On Monday, Toni's office was in chaos. Tuesday was worse. The economy had taken a downturn, and she could have sworn that every investor her company serviced was trying to hedge its losses. The phones never stopped ringing, and when she finally sank behind the wheel of her rented Pontiac—one of these days she had to buy a car—she could still hear the infernal ringing in her ears. If telephones weren't the lifeline of the investment-brokerage business, she would cheerfully rip out every one of them.

Tired as she was, there was one stop to make before she could go home and, as Kyle would say, kick her feet up. She needed a bathing suit, and something wonderful to wear for Kyle's party Saturday night.

The crowds jostling her at the shopping mall did nothing to alleviate her fatigue. And though she managed a wan smile and mumbled, "That's ok," to every "'Scuse me" she heard when someone plowed into her, she was almost gritting her teeth by the time she let herself in the front door.

The sigh of relief preparing to depart from her lips turned into a succinct and very unfeminine expletive. The blasted phone was ringing.

Purse, briefcase and packages tumbled to the floor as she snatched up the nearest phone—the one on the table in the entryway. Her terse, "Hello," was more abrupt than she'd intended.

A warm chuckle on the other end of the line

greeted her. "I had the feeling you'd sound like that."

"Kyle," she breathed, feeling her tension drain away at the sound of his voice. "I don't know why you called, but I'm glad you did. It hasn't been this low in years!" She was talking about the stockmarket.

"I know. You got a lot of people pulling out, or is everyone just trying to cover?"

For the next couple of minutes, their conversation, as it had a tendency to do at times, dealt with the vagaries of their chosen profession. Toni needed Kyle's sympathetic understanding. All day long she'd been dealing with clients who'd made it sound like she was personally responsible for the fact that they were losing their shirts. It was nice to commiserate with someone who'd been subject to those same attacks in the past.

"Enough of that depressing subject," Toni finally said, kicking off her heels. Bracing the phone between her ear and shoulder, she shook off her jacket. "How's your seminar? And why *are* you calling?" He'd never called from out of town before.

"The seminar's going fine. Just the usual strategy stuff. I called because I wanted to remind you to talk to Madeline tomorrow. Be sure to leave her a note to call you at your office."

"I told you not to worry about the party," she chided. "My memory's just as good as it ever was and I hadn't forgotten. Is that the only reason you called?" She had the feeling that it was. It was too much to hope that he might be calling just because he missed her.

She thought he hesitated for a moment, but then decided that he could just as easily have been switching ears.

"Not exactly," he admitted. "I wanted to make sure that you were ok. The way the market's been reminded me of the time that client lost everything he had and threatened to have you burned at the stake for bad advice. You didn't want anyone to know how upset you were, but . . . I just figured you probably had to take a lot of that same kind of guff the past couple of days."

Toni gripped the phone tighter. Dear, sweet Kyle. He had remembered something that had happened over five years ago. "I'm fine," she assured him softly. If he'd been standing in front of her now, nothing would have prevented her from hugging him. His unexpected thoughtfulness had just made the past two days worth every miserable second. It didn't even matter that he was using his old, mentorish tone.

His equally tutorish tone veiled his question. "Are you in for the evening?"

A smile curved her lips as she assured him that she had no intention of leaving the house until morning.

"Good," he pronounced flatly. "You need to stay home alone and unwind."

The key word in that proclamation was "alone," and Toni didn't miss its significance. "I do?" she asked with an innocent inflection.

He ignored her question. "Try the spa. It'll help you relax. Since you don't have a bathing suit, use one of my tee-shirts. They're in the middle-left drawer of my bureau."

Toni's eyes darted to the package lying on the floor, the one containing the sleek, white maillot she'd been lucky to find. Stores in Seattle weren't exactly overstocked with beachwear this time of year.

A mischievous light danced in her eyes. Why tell him she'd just bought a bathing suit? Let him think she was using his hot tub naked. That should help crack that frustrating, brotherly facade! "The spa sounds like a wonderful idea, Kyle. And that's just what I'll do . . . as soon as I get the rest of my clothes off."

That was not subtle, but she might as well take advantage of any situation offered.

Deciding that one more little comment wouldn't hurt—she wanted him to have a very clear picture—her voice lowered seductively. She wondered if she'd be so brave if there wasn't a few hundred miles of phone wire separating them. "I think I'll pass on the tee-shirt. But thanks for the offer. You sure you don't mind my being in your bedroom?"

Dead silence.

"Kyle?"

"Yeah? Uh . . . no, I don't mind."

"You sure?"

She could almost see his jaw clenching as he muttered a curt, "Of course I'm sure."

"Well, I wouldn't want to . . ."

"Look," he broke in, covering what sounded suspiciously like agitation with his brisk, businesslike tone, "I've got to meet a couple of guys down in the bar in a minute. Make a reservation somewhere and I'll buy you that dinner I owe you."

"Why don't we just have dinner here?" She was already planning on that. "You're probably tired of restaurants anyway."

"I said, I'll *buy* your dinner."

Toni couldn't keep the smile from her voice. He did sound a little upset. Not much. But enough. "Have it your way, Donovan," she said, placatingly, knowing that nothing was going to change her own plans. "See you Friday."

Dropping the receiver back on its hook, she scooped her packages, purse and briefcase from the floor. Her smile turned to a full-blown grin.

The market might be down. But Toni wasn't.

Toni was standing in the kitchen, alternating sips of Scotch with prayers that her nerve wouldn't desert her, when she heard the front door open.

Kyle was home. She could hear him moving down the hallway to his bedroom.

Everything had been meticulously planned, right down to the bottle of Pouilly-Fuissé chilling in the ice bucket next to his spa. Dinner would be light—Chicken Kiev, pilaf and fruit. There was a fire burning in the fireplace and soft music playing on the stereo.

The whole scene—especially the spa part—had come straight out of one of Madeline's books. Toni had even had the glass of Scotch the heroine in the novel had needed while setting the stage to lower her hero's defenses. Unlike that imaginary character, Toni wasn't feeling the slightest bit tipsy. She was far too nervous for that.

She didn't look nervous. Years of practice

allowed her anxieties to be masked by sophisticated calm. And as she heard Kyle enter the kitchen she turned to greet him with an easy smile.

Kyle wasn't smiling. He wasn't frowning either. The way the deep grooves bracketing his mouth were deepening, he just looked puzzled. "What's going on?" He had shed his jacket and was working his index finger behind the knot in his tie. "There's a bottle of wine in my bedroom and you . . ."

His words dissolved in a soft expulsion of breath when he finally looked up at her. Cool gray eyes fixed on the smooth fall of hair cascading down her back, then slid the length of the silky white caftan draping her slender curves. He looked like someone had just punched him in the stomach. A fair amount of his color had vanished beneath the collar of his white shirt.

His quickly shuttered eyes darted to the serving platters she had just taken out of the warming oven, and his next words, though even, were very quiet. "It looks like I should have had dinner on the plane."

Tearing her glance from his now enigmatic expression, she redirected it to the platter he was staring at. Oh, geeze, she moaned to herself, I thought he liked chicken!

She glanced back up to see him raking his fingers through his wind-blown hair, and he tossed her a rueful smile. "I used to have a system worked out with my roommate in college," he said, confusing her completely. "If one of us wanted to have some privacy, we'd hang a tie on the outside doorknob. That way the other guy'd know that something was going on inside. Guess we're going to have to devise a similar system, huh?" He pulled his tie from around his neck and she wondered if he was going to hand it to her. He didn't. "In the meantime, I'll get out of your way. How long do I have before he gets here?"

Confusion jerked to understanding. Using her blandest tone, she turned around and reached for the silverware. "The only person I'm expecting is you. So why don't you go get out of your jacket and get comfortable. Do you want a drink before dinner?"

That puzzled look slipped back into his eyes again. "Sure. But I thought we were going out tonight. How come you went to so much trouble?" His head dipped in the general direction of the back of the house. "And what's the wine in by the spa for? And the fire?"

Toni had no pyrotechnic skills at all, and Kyle knew it. Tonight, she had cheated and bought one of those paper and wax wrapped logs at the grocery store. It didn't snap and crackle, but the glow was right.

"I like fires on rainy nights." She shrugged, loading platters and plates on a tray to carry them into the living room. They'd be having dinner in there tonight. "I thought you'd be tired after being out of town all week and might just want to stay home and relax." She ignored his question about the wine.

Kyle seemed to accept her logic, though she didn't miss his thoughtful frown when he followed her out of the kitchen.

She placed the tray on the coffee table and they lowered themselves to the floor, facing the fire. The staging had come from a book. But from here on out, everything was up to her—and Kyle.

He wasn't cooperating.

She had spent fifteen minutes creating the softly romantic lighting. She'd played with the dimmer switch for the recessed lights in the ceiling until the perfect enhancement for the flickering gold fire had been achieved. Kyle immediately ruined the effect by getting up and turning on the table lamps.

"I wanted to show you this chart," he explained, pulling his briefcase down with him as he settled beside her again. He plopped a graph between their plates, and Toni stared at it balefully. If she had looked up, she would have seen how careful he was to keep his suspicious smile hidden. "You've worked with this kind of thing before and . . ."

All through dinner, which he devoured ravenously while she sat there picking at the mushrooms in her rice, he could only talk about cotton futures, the new Security and Exchange Commission rulings and his blasted chart.

Trying to change the subject hadn't helped. Alluding to how peaceful it was to watch the flames licking at the log in the fireplace had brought nothing but a strange, mysterious little glance and then he'd stabbed another piece of chicken before launching into another dissertation about the market.

Toni sank into silence, nodding at appropriate

intervals. If she didn't do something soon, he'd probably get up and turn on the television when they finished eating.

She was so preoccupied with her next move—and the knot of nerves tangled in her stomach that was the result of Kyle's presence as much as anything else—that she didn't notice how quiet he'd become.

Kyle drained the last of his drink. Shifting slightly, he turned to face her, propping one arm on the coffee table and his other on the sofa. She was only an arm's length away and looked like a disgruntled angel, with her legs tucked up under her and her caftan pooled in soft folds on the floor. Her hair almost touched the floor, too. And the white gold tresses reminded him of the fragile white stuff his mother put on the mantel at Christmas. Angel hair, he smiled to himself.

Watching her fingers toy with the pearl hanging at the base of her throat while she studied the fire, he saw her bottom lip slide between her teeth. She was acting very much like she used to whenever she was faced with a problem she couldn't quite solve. Uncertain, yet determined to come to grips with it. He was almost positive he knew what that problem was.

The signals he'd been picking up from her all evening—longer than that if he was going to be honest with himself—could hardly be misconstrued. He'd have to be as dense as a medieval forest not to realize what she was up to.

His tone was purposefully casual. "What's on your mind, princess?"

Startled blue eyes flew toward him and her

hand fell to her lap. "Ah . . . nothing." She smiled. "I was just listening to you."

"I haven't said anything for the last five minutes." Amusement touched his lips. "Do you want to tell me why you're so nervous?"

"I'm not nervous," she lied, wondering what had given her away.

Kyle told her.

"Anytime you start playing with your necklace, I know that you're anxious about something. And you still haven't told me why you've got a thirty-five-dollar bottle of wine chilling in the other room. Are we supposed to be celebrating some . . ." His eyebrows lowered as a flicker of doubt shadowed his features. "You didn't find a house while I was gone, did you?"

He didn't look pleased, which pleased Toni enormously.

"I hardly had time to look for a place," she commented, injecting the proper note of dryness into her tone. Telling herself that it was now or never, she drew herself to her feet. "And the wine was on sale." That hardly explained why it was sitting in the ice bucket by his spa, but she couldn't exactly come right out and tell him why it was there. If he didn't start getting the message soon though, she just might have to.

Kyle watched her lean over to put the dishes on the tray, her hair spilling over her shoulder. He wanted to push it back, run its softness through his fingers. But he didn't. He had to be certain that he wasn't misinterpreting what seemed so obvious. There was only one way to do that.

Her fingers were trembling as she reached for an empty glass.

Pulling himself up beside her, he took the glass from her hand and pressed her palm between his. He felt her stiffen, then relax as she tipped her head back to look up at him.

"Ok, kid," he prodded, forcing his eyes not to wander to her mouth, that beautiful, seductive mouth, "talk."

"About what?"

"About whatever it is that's on your mind."

Her long lashes formed feathery crescents as she looked down at their hands. It wasn't her imagination. His thumb was actually moving back and forth across her wrist. That was not a brotherly gesture. "And if I don't feel like talking?"

"You will," he assured her confidently. "We'll go open that unexplained bottle of wine and then you'll talk to me. Alcohol loosens tongues, you know?" Dropping her hand, he jammed his into his pockets. "Meet me in my room in two minutes."

Something in his voice was giving her the confidence that had been flagging only moments ago. "Is that an order?"

"Absolutely."

"And what if I . . ."

His eyes narrowed in teasing challenge. "Don't push it, Collins. Two minutes. My room."

Two minutes later, Toni hadn't moved from where she had sat down on the arm of the sofa. She had finished the rest of her drink though.

"Toni?" Kyle's voice cut through the walls

separating them. "Your time's up. And bring a corkscrew."

Stuffing her hand into her pocket, her fingers folded over a corkscrew and a tortoiseshell comb. A half-dozen deep breaths and a thousand frantic heartbeats later, she stood somewhat hesitantly on the black tiles surrounding the equally black hot tub. Kyle was already in it.

She couldn't see anything but a froth of foaming water below the flat male nipples on his chest. His broad shoulders glistened in the diffused lighting of the steamy plant-filled room, and his arms were slung out, resting on the lip of the curving tub.

Another steadying breath and she tossed him the corkscrew. The muscles of his arms and chest constricted smoothly with his effortless move to catch it.

He mumbled something that sounded like, "Nice throw," and missed the funny little moan that weighted her throat.

Toni was fine as long as her fingers were occupied with the task of twisting her hair up and securing it with the comb. At least that's what she was telling herself. Kyle wasn't looking at her anyway. He was studying the label on the wine.

"I put a tee-shirt on my bed for you," he said absently.

She didn't acknowledge him—and her fingers felt a little shaky as she reached for the zipper of her caftan and began to pull it down.

Kyle glanced up and his gaze fastened on her hand.

It seemed to take an inordinate amount of effort for him to meet her watchful eyes.

The look on his face and his remark about the tee-shirt told Toni that he remembered that she didn't have a bathing suit.

Making the most of the moment, she let the silky fabric fall slowly to a puddle at her feet.

Chapter Six

$\mathcal{K}$yle's jaw sagged in disappointment; his eyes closed in relief. Quite predictably, that crazy combination of reactions vanished with the slow blink of his lashes.

"Need a hand?" he asked blandly, standing up to extend his as she moved to the step beside him.

Keeping her eyes on the step so she wouldn't slip and do something totally graceless, she felt rather than saw Kyle watching her ankles, calfs and thighs disappear into the warm water. She felt his eyes continue upward. The top of her white maillot was quite modest—no sense calling any attention to her lesser attributes—but the high, French cut of its legs made her legs appear even longer.

Toni lifted her head to smile up at him, but he had already let go of her hand and turned around to open the wine.

"Seventy-nine was a good year for this."

She was staring at the shadow of his dark, and very brief, swim trunks below the water line and was following the indentation of his spine upward to his broad shoulders. Michaelangelo couldn't have sculpted the male anatomy more perfectly.

"I'm sorry," she mumbled to his back. She couldn't seem to make her eyes move. "What did you say?"

"The wine. The Mâconnais district produced an excellent white Burgundy in '78 and '79."

"Excellent," she swallowed.

There was something very compelling about the way the rivulets of water traced the outline of his hard muscles, and the way those wide shoulders tapered to such a tight little . . . She gave her head a shake. The hot water must be making her a little fuzzy, and she needed to keep her wits about her.

He turned around, and her glance fell on the purplish bruise on his left side. With forced ease, she raised her eyes to his. "Does it still hurt?"

It was impossible not to know what she was talking about.

"Only when I laugh," he commented dryly.

"Then I guess we'll have to stick to serious subjects."

"Is the subject you wanted to talk about all that serious?"

"I'm not the one who wanted to talk. That was your idea."

Though amusement curved his firm mouth at her pointed reminder, Kyle was watching her intently. Toni couldn't tell if it was the powerful jet she was standing next to, or the way he was looking at her, that caused the odd, surging sensations she was experiencing at the moment.

"Why don't you tell me what you had in mind then?" he suggested.

She opened her mouth to speak. But quickly closed it again and jerked her eyes to the bubbles breaking rapidly on the surface of the water.

Taking her by the shoulders, Kyle pushed her down onto the bench molded into the spa and handed her one of the filled goblets. "Down the hatch," he ordered. "By the time you finish your half of the bottle, Uncle Kyle will have pried it out of you."

Something in his tone made his obvious reminder of how he viewed their relationship sound strangely like a test. And Toni had the uncomfortable feeling that the tables were turning somehow.

"You're not my uncle," she stated, taking a sip of the wine she didn't want.

"Ok. Brother Kyle, then."

"That makes you sound like a monk. And you're not my brother either."

Though her tone was mildly teasing, there was no humor in her eyes. There was in Kyle's though. "I didn't mean it literally," he defended.

"Did it ever occur to you that I don't want you to mean it figuratively either?"

She had spoken the words quickly, knowing that if she'd hesitated at all, she would have lost her nerve. All she could do now was watch while he sat down a couple of feet away. That, and hold her breath.

Kyle absently tasted his wine, tipping the glass to thoughtfully study its pale clarity. Toni thought her lungs would explode if he didn't say something soon.

He took another sip and directed his question to the stem of his goblet. "Does this mean I've been disinherited?"

The air slid between her teeth in a soft rush. Was the man *trying* to be obtuse? Or did that particular trait come naturally?

She'd give it one last shot. If this didn't work . . .

Her courage must be born of love. She'd never have the nerve to do this otherwise.

Placing her glass on the lip of the tub, she glanced over his shoulder. There were two little buttons behind him. One was for the Jacuzzi-type jets, and the other controlled the aerator that caused the turbulent bubbles. "You don't mind if I turn this off, do you? It's sort of noisy."

Not waiting for a response, she leaned across him, flattening her breasts against his chest and draping her arm over his shoulder. One quick tap of her finger and the bubbles disappeared.

She felt his chest expand as he inhaled sharply, and a thousand little shocks darted through her. He didn't move. But his expression remained frustratingly blank.

"Is that better?" he asked, his eyes following his hand while he raised the glass again. He took another swallow, then pronounced, "This really is very good."

She stifled a defeated moan. Here she was draped across him like a sacrificial mermaid, and all he was interested in was the blasted wine!

Well, she'd done everything she could think of short of attacking him, and she wasn't about to make a bigger fool of herself than she already had.

Her knee rested against the side of his hip. She had to push against him to maintain her balance as she pulled away—or started to pull away. His other hand had settled on her thigh.

"You didn't answer me." Kyle set his glass down, leaving his arm draped over the edge of the spa. "I asked you if it was better."

Her throat felt tight. "It's quieter with the aerator off." She felt his fingers move upward on her thigh, stilling when they settled on her hip. The water was warm, but the skin beneath his hand felt much warmer.

"I'm not talking about the spa equipment."

"I am," she said, trying to defend herself.

"No, you're not. And I think you might as well tell me just what it is that you want."

She was drowning. Not in the heated water gently surging around them, but in the liquid depths of his smoky gray eyes. His gaze fell to her mouth.

"I just . . ." The words stuck. She lowered her head, unable to meet the demand in his expression. There were droplets of water shimmering through the dark hairs on his chest, and she could see the pulse beating at the base of his strong neck.

For someone who never hesitated when it came to juggling millions of dollars, who took on risks and attacked matters with aggression, she was definitely lacking in those assertive traits now.

"You just . . . ?" Kyle prompted.

Her voice was thready, and faint. "I . . . just wanted you to . . . hold me."

A soft whisper of breath tickled her forehead, and she felt his hand drift over her hip as his arm slid around her back. "Come here."

Toni could scarcely breathe. The buoyancy of the water allowed him to lift her easily, and he settled her on his lap. His forearm stayed securely around her back, his hand folded over her stomach. An enervating flutter began to radiate downward from there. With his free hand, he coaxed her head to his shoulder, then allowed his fingers to rest on the side of her neck.

"We all need to be held at times, princess." His lips brushed her brow. "But is that all you want?"

His last words were nothing more than a whisper. Toni didn't hear them over the pounding of her heart, and the beat of Kyle's echoing in her ear. This is where she wanted to be. This is what she had dreamed of. Just being held by him. It would be enough, for now.

A soft whimpering sound escaped from her throat, and his thumb slid over to still the one that followed.

Kyle was barely aware of the soft kisses he was raining in her hair, conscious only of her fingers wending through the wet curls on his chest and the feel of her shallow breath cooling his heated skin. He would only do what she had asked. He would just hold her—and wait to see what she might do.

Toni tipped her head back, the blue of her eyes almost hidden by the heavy fringe of her lashes. Her lips were parted and looked so soft. Kyle felt dazed. Like everything had just taken on some unreal quality that made rationality an unwanted intruder. There was no mistaking what she wanted. At the moment, that was all he wanted, too.

Her eyes closed as his hand folded over her breast, and his lips lowered to hers.

She was kissing him back. Inviting him into the sweet warmth of her mouth. He deepened the kiss, tangling his tongue with hers and encouraging the tiny, mewing sounds buried in her throat. She leaned against his hand, compelling the gentle manipulation of his fingers. Even with the heat of the water swirling around them, and through the flimsy fabric covering her, he could feel her nipple hardening.

Reluctantly he moved his hand.

A soft moan of protest was muffled against his mouth. "It's ok," he whispered, kissing the corner of her mouth and the smooth skin behind her ear. "I only want to take this off."

The ties of her maillot fell away and he drew the fabric down to reveal the gentle swell of her breasts.

Her eyes were wide and the most incredible shade of aquamarine he had ever seen. There was pleading in those languorous depths, a silent request for acceptance that he found so unnecessary.

Splaying his fingers around her waist, he turned her to face him. The huskiness in his voice was enhanced by the feel of her as her knees settled on either side of his hips. Drawing his hands slowly up her sides, feeling the tremors shimmering through her, he cupped her breasts, taunting their rigid tips with his thumbs. "You're perfect, princess," he assured quietly, grazing one tight, umber aureole and then the other before looking back up.

Her head was above his, and her fingers lay curled over his shoulders. Slowly her head lowered and he met that enchanting mouth.

The dull throbbing between his legs escalated to a demanding ache when she arched toward him. Following the line of her throat, his mouth covered one of the hard buds, rolling its tip with his tongue. Her skin tasted like honey, and with each flick of his tongue her sweetness made him crave even more.

Never had Toni allowed a man to touch her so intimately. Never had she dreamed how wonderfully bewildering the sensations he was evoking could be. She wanted Kyle to feel everything she was feeling, to know the love that guided her unpracticed caresses and fueled the desires he was creating within her.

Stroking her fingers through his hair, she kissed its softness, then traced a path with her lips to his shoulder. Tactile senses merged with less definable ones. He tasted warm, and his skin felt like satin, and steel.

His hands were on her waist again, and his lips claimed hers. She felt him drawing her down to his hardness. Something hot coiled inside her, a tension so foreign that she couldn't begin to identify it. When his hips thrust forward, pressing his masculinity against the fabric separating them, she felt that heat become a deep, pulsing ache. Unconsciously, she imitated his slow, erotic rocking motion, unwilling to acknowledge the threat of feminine fear tensing her body. She had nothing to fear. Kyle would . . .

"My God, Toni," he rasped, his fingers digging into the small of her back. "Slow down!"

She hadn't been prepared to cope with the insistent demands of her body. Those demands fought her, begged her to ignore the words that penetrated the sensual fog holding her in its misty grasp. But his last words had been spoken too emphatically to be avoided, and he was pushing her away.

He edged her toward his knees, and she saw her own needs mirrored in his beautifully tortured expression.

"Is this what you had in mind when you asked me to hold you?"

If it hadn't been for the desire so evident in his voice, he might have sounded teasing.

Toni's own voice, that husky contralto, was deeper than usual, too. "Not quite."

Who was she trying to kid? It was exactly what she'd had in mind!

Tracing the fullness of her bottom lip with his finger, he whispered, "So what do you propose we do now?"

He had told himself that she would have the

choice. She had started this, and he'd thought that he'd leave it up to her to dictate how it would end.

Her hesitation made him change his mind.

Picking up the strings of her top floating between them, he tied them around her neck. She still hadn't answered him, not verbally anyway. But the message in her eyes was clear.

She wanted him.

"It's getting late," he said, forcing his own desires behind a mask of controlled indifference.

He wanted her. Toni was just as certain of that as she was her own name. His shuttered expression didn't fool her one bit.

"You're right," she managed with a tremulous smile. "It is getting late."

Not another word was said as he helped her out of the spa, handed her one of the towels from the bench, and watched her pad quickly through his bedroom to hers.

Kyle headed straight for the shower.

It was Saturday. Since it was also only a little after nine in the morning, that meant that Madeline would be working in the kitchen, and Kyle would be downstairs working out.

Toni could hear pots and pans rattling in the sink as she headed toward the kitchen. She'd have a quick cup of coffee with Madeline—if Kyle was on schedule this morning, he wouldn't be upstairs for at least half an hour—and then she'd leave for the office. She didn't trust herself to see him yet. The wistful smile clinging to her lips simply didn't want to go away, and that would be far too revealing.

Her memories of what had happened last night had given way to her wonderful old dream. It had seemed so real, and in her mind she could still see his smile of adoration as she floated toward him in a billowing white gown while an organ played and the scent of orange blossoms filled . . .

She gave her head a shake and dropped her briefcase on the entryway table. She'd made progress last night. But not *that* much! And right now, she'd be better off thinking about the Westline Clinic account.

That thought effectively removed her smile. It was going to be a while before she could implement her decision not to work on weekends anymore. This business of working six and seven days a week was definitely beginning to lose its former appeal.

"Morning." Toni directed her greeting to the skirt of her winter white wool dress and flicked a piece of lint from the pleat. Tossing her matching jacket on the counter, she smiled up at . . . Kyle. Rather, his back. He was standing at the sink.

Thank God that dumb, misty grin wasn't plastered on her face anymore!

"Morning," he returned, not bothering to turn around. "Coffee's ready."

Toni headed for the cupboard, watching him through her lowered lashes. "Where's Madeline this morning?"

"At the store." He turned off the water he'd

been running into a large saucepan—Madeline had already been busy with more preparations for tonight's party—and dried his hands on the towel he'd flipped over his shoulder. "I got left in charge of KP. You have an appointment?"

Toni drowned her vague sense of disappointment with a sip of coffee. It was normal conversation. Depressingly normal.

With an inward sigh, she glanced down at her dress. She knew what had prompted his question. Usually, she wore slacks to the office on weekends. "Actually . . ." She picked up his empty mug from beside the coffeepot, silently asking if he wanted more by lifting it toward him. He nodded. ". . . I have a couple of appointments. They're not until this afternoon though, and I thought I'd spend the morning trying to find my desk. The last I saw of it, it was buried under a pile of computer printouts."

She handed him his cup. Only the slight pinch of her eyebrows indicated that she'd noticed how carefully he'd avoided touching her fingers.

"When will you be home?"

"By five or so . . . I hope." Her blue eyes swept cautiously to his face. He looked tired. "Why?"

"Just curious. How did you sleep?"

He was watching her over the rim of his mug.

It was a simple question. Rather like asking someone how they were and expecting nothing more than an equally simple, "Fine."

Toni knew that he wasn't just making idle conversation though.

"Ok, I guess." She held his unblinking gaze steadily. "And you?"

Cat and mouse. It was an unusual game for them to play.

Kyle's gray eyes were deliberately traveling the length of her body, their depths unrevealing when they returned to her slightly flushed features. "I've slept better," he informed her dryly.

Toni's small surge of triumph—if he was losing sleep because of her, she was definitely getting somewhere!—was interrupted by the doorbell.

She didn't quite understand his taunting smile as he took another sip of coffee, then announced that "Madeline's back."

Kyle willingly complied with Madeline's request that he stay out of her way, and threw himself into a sweat-inducing workout on the weight machine.

The Toni he'd known five years ago no longer existed. Somewhere along the line she'd been cured of that delusive Pollyanna innocence. In many ways, he liked her better without it, or so he told himself. She had clearly given up all of those idiotic romantic notions she used to have. And after last night, it was obvious enough that she had no compunction about adding sex to their relationship. So, why not take advantage of what she was offering? There was no denying that he wanted her!

Hell, he corrected, his muscles straining as he fought the resistance of the machine's hydraulic system. He *ached* for her!

His need for Toni was more than physical though. She was becoming more important to him every day. If they had an affair, she'd become even more important. Then what would he do?

Marriage was out of the question. If Toni had become the person he thought she had, she wasn't interested in it anyway. But was risking the loss of their friendship worth it for something that could never lead anywhere? Affairs had to end, didn't they? And what about the other men in her life?

Kyle didn't have the answers.

His last question presented itself again several hours later. It was seven-thirty and his guests had already started to arrive. Toni still wasn't home.

Kyle had just opened the door to greet another couple, when he saw the silver Mercedes pull into the drive. He recognized that car immediately—as well as the man behind the wheel.

The driver of that car was Dr. Greg Nichols. And Toni was with him.

The couple Kyle turned toward saw nothing of the strain behind their host's welcoming smile.

The schedule Toni had planned for the day had fallen apart right after her first meeting. Who would ever have thought that her last appointment would take four hours? Or that her rental car would pick this particular Saturday to develop a temperament?

"Thanks, Greg," she said, picking up her briefcase from the floorboard and opening the passenger door of his car. She glanced toward the house. The driveway was full of cars, and they'd passed at least two dozen more parked along the street. "I appreciate the ride."

Greg nodded his curly blond head and flashed her a glimpse of his even white teeth. The dark tan he'd acquired during the medical conference he'd just returned from in Hawaii, and his imported cashmere sweater in a shade of green that matched his eyes perfectly, hardly helped promote the image of a struggling young doctor. Struggling and young were his terms. He was almost forty and, being quite familiar with his financial statements, Toni knew that his only struggle was one for tax shelters.

"No problem," he returned amiably. "How about dinner some night this week?"

The invitation was casual. Probably an attempt to return the favor she had just done him by presenting the investment package *he* wanted to his associates. That's what they'd been discussing all afternoon.

"Sounds fine." She swung her legs out the door. "We can talk about converting those gas bonds into the stocks I mentioned earlier."

"Good idea. I'll call you the first part of the week to set something up."

Toni let herself out of the car and headed up the walkway. She enjoyed working with Greg. Their business relationship was a good one. It was too bad that Kyle nearly turned green every time he heard Greg's name. Too bad, and very flattering.

The laughter coming from inside the house greeted her before she even reached the front door. The party was well underway. Somehow she had to make it to her room without attracting anyone's attention—especially Kyle's.

The Fates were with her. Breathing an excited sigh as she burst through the door of her room, she headed straight for the closet.

Kyle had made that comment about her legs when he'd subjected her to that nerve-wracking massage her first Saturday here. He'd also asked her to wear a dress for this party.

Well, she smiled to herself, stepping back out into the hall twenty minutes later. If he wants to see legs, he most definitely will. Along with a flash of thigh and a bared back.

The halter-style skim of toast-colored crepe brushing her knees had cost a small fortune. Considering the possible return on her investment, it was worth every penny.

With her hair knotted in a sleek French twist, the gold squares adorning her ears, and the carmel-toned pumps accentuating the long line of her legs, she was all honey and cream and sultry turquoise eyes bright with anticipation. Cool sophistication wrapped around a bundle of nerves.

Kyle had invited some sixty-odd people. Though she knew that a lot of the guests were downstairs, she could have sworn that most of them were packed into the spacious living room. There may have been over thirty people there, but her eyes unerringly fixed on Kyle.

He was standing by the wet bar talking to a group of men. His back was to her, but even with the crowd separating them, she could feel the impact of his presence. Odd how one person could affect her so when she was surrounded by so many others.

"Toni?"

The question that accompanied her name was to become a familiar sound within the next hour. She never did reach Kyle. Since he hadn't appeared at her side either, she was almost certain that he didn't even know she'd come home.

Most of the guests were people Toni had known from years ago. People she used to work with and clients of Kyle's company. Her conversations were polite, her smile genuine. But her eyes were constantly seeking the one person who seemed to have disappeared completely.

It was while she was still looking for Kyle that she spotted Jana Rand standing by the sofa. The tiny brunette looked like she was about to deck the bald man talking to her cleavage. Toni and Jana had only spoken briefly—they were old "lunch buddies"—and Toni decided that now was as good a time as any to have the little talk they had promised each other. Jana might also know where Kyle was.

Snagging two glasses of wine from the bar, she cut her way through the crowd.

"Do you have a minute, Jana?" Toni extended one of the glasses to her and was blessed with relief in the woman's wide hazel eyes.

"Do I ever," Jana breathed.

Toni smiled tightly at the glassy-eyed man she recognized as an old client of Kyle's. Both women ignored his sputtered, "Hey, baby, where ya going?" as they moved out to the deck.

The night was cool, almost cold, but the people

lining the redwood railing either didn't notice or didn't care.

Todd Ruger, looking considerably cleaner than he had at the football game, materialized from somewhere beside them. "Hi, ladies!"

"Don't take this personally"—Jana winked at Toni, then looked up at her co-worker—"but since you have the misfortune of being a male, I don't think we want to talk to you."

Todd's smile faltered, his glance jerking from one woman to the other.

"Oh, stop looking like a wounded puppy," Jana muttered, taking a cigarette from her purse and lighting it. "I was only kidding." She exhaled a puff of smoke. "Thanks for the rescue, Toni."

"What rescue?" Todd's eyes were still darting back and forth.

"From Larry the Leerer," Toni supplied, referring to the man who'd been practically salivating down the front of Jana's blouse.

Todd was frowning. Jana laughed. "Larry Norman," she clarified. "The lech of the Northwest's Wall Street."

Todd's boyish features split in a grin. "And the ink isn't even dry yet."

It was Toni's turn to look puzzled, but Jana's quick response answered her unspoken question.

"I guess it's something I'll have to get used to. I'd swear that all men think it's open season on any woman who's about to join the ranks of the single."

Jana was apparently getting a divorce. Toni

had attended her wedding. "I'm sorry, Jana," she said quietly.

The small woman pushed back a handful of her dark brown curls and squinted through the haze of smoke. "Me, too."

Todd had gone through a divorce a couple of years ago—he'd told Toni that at the game—and she took his silence now for empathy.

Unwilling to let that silence become acute, she glanced up at her companions. "Have either of you seen Kyle?"

It was Jana who answered. "The last I saw of him, he was headed downstairs. Shall we go find him?"

"No, that's ok. I just haven't seen him yet and . . ."

"You're about to." Jana was nodding toward the doorway.

Before the words had even left Jana's mouth, Toni felt the fine hairs on the back of her neck begin to prickle. That slightly unnerving sensation traveled down her bare back, and it was impossible not to shiver. Her eyes, eager for the sight of the only man who could have evoked such a reaction, darted over her shoulder.

Kyle stepped into the space between her and Todd.

"Hi," she managed softly.

"Hi, yourself," he returned. His mouth curved upward, but his smile didn't quite reach his eyes. He glanced from Todd to Jana. "Am I interrupting anything interesting?"

Toni hadn't expected anything more than his perfunctory greeting. After all, this party really was a business function. And Kyle was always the same around his business associates. Reserved. Coolly aloof. He could be very intimidating if he wanted to. Or like now, appear friendly without ever allowing anyone to see behind that unemotional facade.

His manner now was a striking reminder of the Kyle she had first come to know.

"Heavens no," Jana was replying to his question. "We were just about to discuss the perils and pitfalls of marriage, which car manufacturer will get the next government subsidy, and who's going to drop the first nuclear bomb."

There was something about Jana that prevented her words from sounding bitter. Maybe it was the sad smile that never seemed to leave her eyes. Or the sense of strength packed into her petite frame. Whatever it was, Toni couldn't help but admire her. Her world was probably falling apart, and she was still able to poke fun at it.

"I'm all for light conversation." Kyle crossed his arms over his tailored gray suit jacket. He looked wonderful in gray. "So let's start with cars. Where's yours, Toni?"

His expression revealed nothing. But Toni didn't need any brilliant flashes of recognition to realize that he must have seen Greg bringing her home.

"In the parking lot at Westline Clinic with a short or something." There was really no need for further explanation, and it was only for the benefit of the others that she continued. Kyle already knew about the Westline account. "I was there to meet with some investors . . . a group of doctors . . . and when I left, it wouldn't start. One of the doctors brought me home."

Todd's eyebrow raised at her last word. Toni ignored its significance and, with a laugh meant only to mock her procrastination, she added, "It's a rental anyway, and I suppose that tomorrow will be as good a time as any to start looking for one to buy."

The funny expression on Todd's face told Toni that he wasn't interested in her car problems. "You said he brought you home? Here?"

Toni's eyes darted to Kyle. His private life had been a constant source of speculation among his employees, and apparently still was. It was also apparent that Kyle hadn't mentioned their living arrangement. She'd leave it up to him to answer Todd.

His bland tone indicated that he wasn't particularly displeased with this invasion of his privacy—or hers. "Toni lives with me . . . just in case you were interested."

Kyle was looking at Todd. Todd and Jana were both looking at Toni. She didn't know why she felt the need to undo Kyle's seeming implication. Unless it had something to do with the fact that, as openminded as she told herself she was, she was still saddled with a few Victorian principles. "I've been staying here for the last few weeks," she said evenly, taking an unhurried sip of her wine. "I haven't had time to find a place of my own yet, and Kyle's out of town a lot."

"Not that often," Kyle commented tonelessly. "Can I have one of your cigarettes, Jana?"

Toni's brow creased. Both at his request—he'd

said he'd quit smoking three years ago—and at his heavily suggestive words. It wasn't until she saw the look Kyle slanted at Todd when he touched his cigarette to Jana's lighter that Toni realized what he was doing.

Kyle was making it very clear to Todd that she was off limits.

Any embarrassment she might have been feeling was forgotten, and she suppressed a smile of delight. It was too early to congratulate herself over any victories yet. But she was definitely making some positive inroads.

She was about to capitalize on her progress—a veiled little comment certainly wouldn't hurt—when Jana suddenly ducked behind Todd's bear-like frame.

"Oh, God," Jana moaned. "Larry's coming out here. I swear that man's got a one-track mind."

"Men don't have an exclusive corner on that market," Todd laughed, pulling Jana around. "And you can let go of my jacket. He went back inside."

Toni's amusement at their exchange wavered as she turned to Kyle. He was looking at her very strangely.

Jana and Todd were still bantering about something. But Toni didn't hear them. She was too busy trying to fathom what she was seeing in those enigmatic gray depths. It was almost as if he were accusing her of some unspoken transgression.

How can she look so innocent? Kyle asked himself while she stood there holding his gaze. She's got half the men in this place drooling like

Pavlov's dogs, and she doesn't even look like she cares!

His eyes raked over her dress, then settled hard on her face. No doubt about it. Toni had definitely changed.

That unveiled inspection told Toni quite plainly what the problem was. Her dress was provocative, but no more so than most of the other women's—and she doubted that he was treating *them* to any searing looks of disapproval!

With a kittenish grin, she turned back to the others.

". . . have to stick to what really counts," Todd was saying. "Forget about involvements for a while, and just concentrate on work. At least that's always there to fall back on."

The conversation was preparing to settle on a more serious topic. "You're right." Jana nodded thoughtfully. "Doing what we do for a living doesn't give you time to think about much of anything else . . . at least between the ungodly hours of 5:00 A.M. to whenever you can finally get away."

"Just remember to keep your priorities straight, Jana," Kyle warned. "You've got that little girl to think about."

Toni was touched at Kyle's concern. What caused her heart to take a funny lurch, though, wasn't that concern. It was the odd note she had detected in his voice when he'd mentioned Jana's daughter.

Kyle's expression remained quite unremarkable as he continued, now going on about transferring some of Jana's accounts to the other brokers so she wouldn't have to make after-hours appointments. That distracting note was gone, but it had brought a question to Toni's mind that she couldn't ignore.

Did Kyle have a child somewhere?

That question prompted others. About his ex-wife who might have taken that child from him. About whether that loss was the reason he had always had such a dismissive attitude toward kids. She remembered the way he had acted around Todd's son, the obvious affection and the quick disinterest. Then she shoved those thoughts to the back of her mind to be dealt with later. She couldn't think about them now anyway. Todd had just spoken her name. Again.

"I'm sorry." She smiled apologetically. "I got sidetracked. What did you say?"

"I asked what you thought about Kyle's comment. You used to have some . . . well . . . let's just call them firm opinions."

Kyle repeated himself at her expectant expression. "I was just saying that I didn't think that Jana was in any danger of this happening, but that some women get pretty wrapped up in some romantic notion about riding off into the sunset with their knight in shining armor . . . and when he falls off his horse, they wind up taking their frustrations out by hiding in their work and a bunch of empty affairs."

The teasing light in his eyes masked any provocation. Toni couldn't see anything pointed in his remarks anyway. She'd never had an empty affair in her life. She'd never had an affair, period!

"I can see where that might happen," she

returned comfortably. "Sometimes we get so wrapped up in our dreams that we find it easier to run away than face the fact that what we want just isn't there." She wasn't talking about herself. Her approach was strictly philosophical. Cocktail conversation had a tendency to edge in that direction sometimes. "An extremely idealistic person might find cold reality a little difficult to face and, in trying to cope with that reality, might go overboard and wind up abandoning the attitudes that got them into their predicament in the first place."

"Psychology 101," Todd taunted good-naturedly. "I think I had a professor that talked like that."

Jana piped in. "There's nothing wrong with being a little idealistic. It can't ever hurt to keep the dreams in mind even though we've found 'cold reality' to be a little disillusioning."

Toni couldn't help but think that Jana was talking about her failed marriage. Something in Kyle's guarded expression told her that he was thinking of something quite specific, too.

"Oh, yes," he replied, crushing out his cigarette. "We must remember the dreams. If it weren't for them, we wouldn't be where we are now . . . whether or not they ever came true."

There was no reason for Toni to think that Kyle was doing anything other than adding his two cents' worth to the conversation. Still, she couldn't help wondering if, somewhere beneath his casual words, there wasn't a little zinger trying to find its mark. He used to get a kick out of pulling her into a discussion, setting her up with innocuous statements, and then landing the line that would leave her fumbling for a defense. There was nothing malicious about it. They had become friends baiting each other that way. It had taken Toni a while to catch on to his tactics. Once the lesson had been learned though, she'd had her share of verbal victories.

She didn't even realize that he had already delivered the punchline. He had buried it in his remark about the "empty affairs" and was marveling at how she hadn't even batted an eye.

Jana and Todd were carrying the conversational ball now, and Kyle leaned toward her. The smooth wool of his jacket felt surprisingly rough against her bare arm, the pressure of his harder one sensitizing her skin. "I think I'll leave you in charge of this little discussion."

It wasn't until he touched her that she realized how hard it had been to maintain her casual air. His words were anything but intimate. Still, the rapid darkening in his eyes as they fell to her mouth made it evident that her presence was taking its toll on him, too.

Despite the quick tightening in her throat, she managed lightly, "Think I can handle it?"

His jaw clenched beautifully. "I'm not sure if I can." He stepped behind her, his breath tickling her hair as he leaned to whisper in her ear. "Don't plan on going to bed right after everyone leaves. You and I have something to talk about."

The shudder of anticipation at his husky command was echoed again when she felt his hand brush her back. She swung around, wanting to see if his expression revealed what she had heard in his voice. All she saw was his back before he was swallowed up by the crowd inside.

It was probably just as well that she hadn't seen his expression just then. She was nervous enough for the remainder of the evening without having to puzzle over why he had looked so angry.

She never did see that anger. Kyle buried it. And it joined all the other emotions he told himself he wasn't feeling. Jealousy. Protectiveness. And something else he didn't want to name.

As the evening wore on, Toni found herself plagued with a previously unacknowledged set of anxieties. Ones she adamantly refused to think about. She laughed at Todd's sick jokes—wondering why she actually found some of them funny. Heard all about Carol Gray's new job in Denver—it sounded quite familiar and Toni offered her sympathies. Endured a heated debate over the future of the American Football League —boring. And tried not to think about Kyle.

He was ignoring her. Quite pointedly.

Her mental powers of denial finally crumbled somewhere between her second glass of soda water and someone's offer of a Swedish meatball. She refused the latter. The knot in her stomach wouldn't allow room for anything else.

Kyle had said he wanted to talk. What if he said something she didn't want to hear? What if he was going to tell her that last night had been a mistake and that they could never be more than just friends? Why did he look away from her every time she met his eyes?

Dwelling on questions that couldn't be answered at the moment was fruitless, so she dove into the conversation she'd been listening to.

The only thing threatening about the discussion of mutual funds was the fact that Kyle's eyes on her back kept making her forget what she was talking about.

It seemed like forever before the last guest finally left. In another way, it seemed like everyone left too soon.

Chapter Seven

$\mathcal{K}$yle leaned against the door, his dark eyes fixed on Toni's carefully controlled features. Anyone who didn't know her would think that her self-assured expression held a wealth of confidence.

Kyle knew better. She was playing with her pearl. One of these days he'd ask her why she always wore it.

Toni could see a question forming in Kyle's narrowed gaze, and she steeled herself against it. She didn't want to be on the defensive, but she couldn't help it. Being ignored for most of the evening had had a distinctly adverse effect. Though she'd always thought that the female ego was stronger than the male's, it was hardly indestructible.

She watched quietly when he crossed his arms

and moved to where she was standing by the stairs leading into the living room.

"What are you trying to do to yourself, Toni?"

The flatness in his voice didn't puzzle her anywhere near as much as his question did, and her brow dropped sharply. "What do you mean?"

His cool gray eyes took a deliberately slow journey from her neck to her knees and back up to meet the pulse skipping at the base of her throat. There had been nothing impersonal about his look, yet when his eyes met hers again, there was nothing there but accusation.

"For starters," he returned pointedly. "I'd like to know what happened that made you lose sight of all the things that were so important to you. You used to enjoy your work, but you were never so obsessed with it."

Work? Two seconds ago he was mentally disrobing her and now he wanted to talk about work? The man was impossible!

"I'm hardly obsessed, Kyle," she declared. She gave her pearl a flick, then crossed her arms complacently. There was nothing to be nervous about now. Disappointed. Maybe even relieved. But not nervous. "I think 'obsessed' was a word invented to describe you a few years ago. I never have driven myself into the ground the way you did, and work is hardly my whole life." Not anymore anyway.

"I had my reasons for doing what I did. But we're not talking about me. We're talking about you." The spark in his eyes spoke clearly of challenge. "It's not just how you bury yourself in your job either. The woman I used to know would never have a string of men who . . ."

She had wanted to know what *his* reasons were, and to ask what had happened to make him so different now. His last words sliced cleanly through that intended interruption though and primed another one. "Wait a minute! What men? What are you implying?"

"I'm not implying anything. And I'm not accusing you either. God knows I've never espoused celibacy, but I hate seeing what you're doing to yourself." His tone wasn't exactly altruistic, though it was obvious he was trying to make it sound that way. "I've been there, Collins. And you've got too much going for you to turn into some bitter old woman who winds up with nothing but the memory of a rat-race job and a hundred empty affairs to keep her company in her old age."

Disbelief vied with incomprehension. "What on earth are you talking about?"

"All right," he sighed, assuming a less revealing tone. "You want to do this like we used to? Lay everything out point by point?"

She nodded sharply, refusing to be placated by his more reasonable approach. Anytime Kyle turned reasonable on her in the middle of a discussion, she knew that he had an ace up his sleeve.

"One." He held up a finger. Toni scowled at it. "You spent the day with Greg. Right?"

Oh, Lord, she moaned to herself. "Part of it, but . . ."

"Two." He added another finger. "Last week you were asking me how to get some other guy to notice you. Right?"

So much for her subtle inquiries. "Yes, but . . ."

"Three." Another finger joined the others. "You almost wound up in bed with me last night. Right?"

That was stating it rather bluntly. Toni swallowed hard. "Yes."

She waited for him to present another point. He said nothing though. He just held her eyes steadily, waiting.

"Can I have my turn now?"

His nod was deferential, but Toni saw his hands ball into fists as he crossed his arms. Her own nails were digging into her palms.

"For a reasonably intelligent man," she began, not bothering to temper her terseness, "you've drawn some pretty erroneous conclusions, Donovan." She thought it best to let his remark about her winding up in bed with him slide for the moment. "First of all, there isn't any 'guy.' And as for my becoming an embittered old woman, that's something I have absolutely no intention of letting happen. I'm still the same person I always was and I don't have any deep, dark secrets to reveal." Being in love with you doesn't count, she mentally justified.

Kyle didn't look like he was buying any of this, but the fractional hardening in his eyes told her that he had just homed in on some point she'd made, or tried to make. "What did you say?"

"About what?" Exasperation tinged her tone. "I said a lot of things!"

He took a step closer, struggling against the conclusions he'd drawn and her refuting words.

If she'd meant what he thought she had . . . "About there not being any guy."

"I said that there isn't anyone else."

That's what he thought she'd said. "Meaning?"

"Oh, for cripe sake, Donovan! You're giving new meaning to the word thick-headed! Meaning that I'm not interested in any other man. Certainly not in Greg. And there isn't any mythical, magical male out there that I'm trying to get my claws into!" How much clearer could she get?

"If that's the case, then would you mind explaining what last night was all about?"

Toni saw only the antagonism in his expression. She was too agitated, too exasperated, to notice the devious hint of teasing in his tone. "I was trying to get you to notice me!"

"Notice you?" he repeated incredulously. "You've got to be joking! There's not a damn thing about you that I *don't* notice!"

"Then why have you been making things so 'damn' difficult? If you don't want me, just say so, and I'll stop making a fool of myself!"

Tossing him what she hoped was a challenging glare—she'd pulled some pretty aggressive stunts before, but this one topped the list—she turned away before that feigned confidence could terminate. She didn't feel confident at all. Being aggressive in business didn't hold the same threat as being that way with a man.

She hadn't taken two steps before she felt Kyle's hand gripping the bare skin of her upper arm. A moment later he had stepped in front of her and was watching the uncertainty play over her flustered features. He'd never seen her look that way before.

Kyle stared down at her. And the seconds ticked away one by one.

With each passing second, she could see the strain melting from his face, the beginnings of a smile softening the hard line of his lips.

The pressure of his hand on her arm increased almost imperceptibly, repeating the frisson of tremors that had raced to the tips of her fingers only moments before. His hand raised slowly, her throat tightening when his knuckles grazed her cheek. Mesmerized by the transformation taking place before her, she had to make a concerted effort to breathe when his thumb smoothed the tension from her mouth.

"Do you have any idea how hard it's been for me to keep my hands off of you?" He inched closer. "How many times I've wanted to take you in my arms in the morning and kiss the sleep from your eyes? To just be able to feel you against me?" The tip of his finger pressed to her bottom lip, coaxing it to part, and he continued tracing its inviting texture. "I kept telling myself that we'd be better off to just leave things the way they are. That there was no sense in complicating what we've got. I can't fight both of us anymore, princess. And after last night . . ."

He didn't need to say anything else. It was all there in his eyes.

She could feel his breath on her forehead, its rhythm heavy. Almost as erratic as her own. "It won't complicate anything," she promised, loving the feel of his fingers as they wended through her hair. "We'll just make it better."

His thumbs stroked her temples. "It's already better."

His words were a verbal caress, as seductive as the feel of his hands as he gently pulled the pins from her hair and smoothed the long, flaxen tresses over her back.

"I do want you, Toni," he breathed, his hand delving beneath the white gold veil to press into the small of her back. "I do want you."

His last words were spoken against her lips, their faint vibration lost in the hunger that burst through him in a quiet explosion of need. There was nothing now but the feel of her body, warm and pliant and trembling against his own.

And the feel of his body, hard and demanding against hers. Toni clung to him, needing his strength to stabilize the spinning in her head, the weakness in her legs.

She followed his lead. Her tongue imitating his motions when it flicked over the slick membrane behind his lower lip. Plunging again to taste his warmth. Gently nipping at his tongue before giving up that teasing play to seek more urgently.

Toni's soft moan was suppressed against his chest as he bent forward to lift her. His hand slid beneath the hem of her dress, his palm hot against her thigh. Then his arm was under her knees and his other tightened around her back. She could hear the strong thud of his heart beating twice for every step he took while he carried her down the hall.

She was floating. Lost in a misty world of longing that held only enough room for her and the man whose kisses turned her blood into warm, thick honey. The man who was going to have to teach her how to create that same drugging sensation in him.

Kyle's lips followed the path of his hands, and her dress fell to the floor. Wanting, needing, to touch him as he had her, she repeated his actions. Tremulous kisses were rained over his chest as she removed his shirt, and the rest of his clothes joined hers on the floor.

Driven nearly beyond control by the beautiful, natural way she sought to entice him as he had her, he pushed her down to his circular bed. He tasted the pouting tips of her breasts, the smooth skin of her stomach, the firm flesh of her thighs. Toni rolled him over, returning his caresses, his kisses, with her own.

To Kyle, she was making an erotic game of their lovemaking. A sensual game of follow the leader. Her hands felt like satin. Her lips like hot silk. She was a nymph who toyed with him, taunted him with her sometimes tentative, sometimes bold touches. A woman who knew how to please.

A woman who was being led by her heart. And the man she loved.

Kyle pinned her back to the soft blue sheets and began nibbling moist kisses down her throat, seeking the gentle swell of her breast. As he teased the hard nipple with his teeth, his tongue, she felt his hand moving down to stroke the inside of her legs. Every sensation he had evoked last night paled next to those he was eliciting now. His hand cupped the curls between her thighs, his fingers gently probing. She stiffened involuntarily, her fingers digging into his back.

"You're so tight, honey," he rasped, soothing her with slow, deliberate motions. "So tight and so ready for me."

"Please, Kyle." Her words were a faint whisper. If he didn't stop this exquisite torture soon, she would die with wanting him. "Please," she repeated, and his lips claimed hers again.

Still he didn't stop. She shifted restlessly, gripping the tensed muscles in his shoulders. She wanted to feel his weight on her. To have him teach her where this odd, escalating heat-throbbing where he stroked so boldly would lead.

Kyle knew that she was close. And he couldn't wait any longer.

Sliding his hand beneath her hips, he moved over her. She felt his knees nudging her legs apart as he aligned her feminity to him. She arched upward, instinct guiding her where experience could not, and he sought to fulfill the desires raging within them.

Her gasp was muffled against his mouth. She had tried to silence it, but Kyle heard it anyway. And he knew that it wasn't a groan of pleasure. His body grew rigid, his mind not wanting to comprehend what had suddenly become quite apparent. She had felt tight. Too tight. And now . . .

He started to pull back.

Both his own desires and Toni's hands stopped him.

"No," she pleaded. "Don't stop. Not now."

This time it was Kyle who moaned.

He couldn't have stopped if he'd wanted to. Clamping his mouth over hers in an effort to drink the pain he knew she was feeling, he broke that last resistance and buried himself in her warmth.

He forced himself not to move. To try and ignore the insistent demands of his body. "Are you all right?" There was more than concern revealed in his deep velvet voice.

She nodded. Already the pain was subsiding, giving way to infinitely more pleasurable feelings. "Help me, Kyle?"

The innocence in her question was astounding. Just as incredible as the gift of innocence she had just given him.

"I will, princess," he promised. He kissed her cheek, her eyes. "I will." His hand slid down to her hip. "Wrap your legs around mine, and move with me. That's it. Easy. Nice and . . . easy."

Gently he coaxed her. Guided her. And through the night he taught her the wonderful mysteries of her body. The perfect oneness that is created in that inexplicable moment when conscious thought gives way to an implosion of feeling so intense that nothing else exists. And she learned how to please him.

Toni fought the return of consciousness and snuggled into the warm curve of Kyle's arm. She didn't want to wake up yet. This was a wonderful dream.

"You going to sleep all day?"

"Mmmm," she murmured, curling her fingers against his chest. His chest? Her eyes flew open and she focused on the dark curls visible between her fingers. She wasn't dreaming!

Memories of the beautiful night they had shared shattered her lassitude. Everything was very real. Kyle was here, holding her. She could feel the strong beat of his heart beneath her hand. The feel of denim against her legs.

Denim? Maybe she wasn't quite awake yet.

"If any of your employees could see you now, I think they'd be hard pressed to ever take you seriously." He chuckled and dropped a kiss to her sleep-warmed mouth. "You look like a little kid," he continued, his hand roaming over her rib cage and settling on her hip. "You don't *feel* like a little kid, but you sure do look like one."

The little shocks darting inward from where he was kneading the curve of her hip told her that she was most definitely awake now. Being conscious was one thing. Being articulate when she first woke up was another. So she couldn't tell him that she felt exactly like a child—one who had just received the present she'd been waiting for all of her life on Christmas morning.

She moved her head to rest it on his arm and blinked the sleep from her eyes. Kyle was smiling down at her.

He propped himself up on his elbow and pushed her hair back from her face. "Sunday mornings are great for sleeping in, but it's almost eleven. Aren't you hungry?"

She shook her head. "Coffee."

"It's already on." A rakish grin split his handsome features. "While you've been playing Sleeping Beauty, I've been reading the paper.

I've taken a shower. Shaved." He ran his hand over his smooth jaw. "And I think it's time you got up so we can start prowling car lots. I can think of things I'd rather do"—his hand slid between her legs.—"but you need to take care of your rental car and look for one to buy."

"Kyle!"

"What?"

"Don't!"

"Still limited to one word responses in the morning, huh?"

His hand feathered along the inside of her thigh again.

"That tickles!"

"Two words. Very good. And it's not supposed to tickle."

Despite his suggestive tone, she knew from the teasing in his eyes that that was exactly what it was supposed to do. She tried to scoot away.

Her attempt met with a mock-heavy sigh. "You're right," he conceded, rolling over to sit on the edge of the bed. "We'd better take it easy. How do you feel?"

Why did he sound so serious all of a sudden?

He stood up and she blinked at the pair of well-worn jeans stretched over his lean hips. "I feel fine."

"You might want to wait until you're on your feet to answer that." He held out his hand. "It's possible that you may change your mind."

She hadn't taken his hand, and Kyle smiled at her hesitation. Picking up his robe from the chair, he draped it over her shoulders and pulled her up.

Toni was telling herself that it was silly to worry about modesty now—and silently thanking Kyle for being so understanding—when her feet hit the floor. "Ohh," she groaned, knowing now what had prompted his concern. She ached in places she'd never . . .

"That's what I thought," he mumbled knowingly. Taking her by the arms, he guided her toward his bathroom. "Pardon me for putting this so indelicately, but it's a little like riding a horse. The first few times leave you a little sore, but after that . . ." His words trailed off as she ducked her head. He nudged her chin up with his finger, a tender smile clinging to his mouth. "I don't think I've ever seen you do that before."

"Do what?"

"Blush."

"Oh, stop grinning like that and get out of here so I can get a shower."

"Want company?"

"You said you already took one."

His hand slid beneath the robe. "I'll take another."

"I thought you said we were going to take it easy." She couldn't help the breathy note in her voice any more than she could help the response his provocative caress was eliciting.

Negating any unwillingness he may have detected in her reminder, she curved her arms around his neck.

The robe fell to the floor.

"We will," he breathed against her lips. Cupping her breasts, he trailed a line of hot kisses down her throat. "We will."

I love you, Kyle. Those words had been swallowed back more times than Toni cared to count during the next three days. They were always there, wanting to be spoken. Making her heart feel like it would burst if she didn't give it that release. Oddly enough, it wasn't during their lovemaking that she found it so difficult to keep those words to herself. Then, she could silence them against his lips and transfer those feelings into physical form. It was all the other times in between.

She had choked them back with a gulp of coffee when he'd teased her about forgetting to put cream in it Monday morning. Buried them in the lapel of his jacket when he'd come home Tuesday. Literally bitten her tongue not to say them when they'd come home Sunday afternoon with her new white Audi.

Kyle wasn't ready to hear those words. And she knew that the new bond developing between them was too fragile to withstand that test.

Time, she told herself, negotiating the curve at the top of the hill. *All we need is time.* She pulled her Audi into the drive, and a wide smile broke across her face. Kyle's car was there, and that meant he was home.

Fairly flying up the steps, she assumed a more sedate pace when she reached the entry and headed down the steps into the living room. Kyle was sitting on the sofa. In front of him a stack of files leaned in a lopsided tower on the coffee table.

She bent from behind him, wrapping her arms across his chest, and brushed his cheek with her lips. "I thought you said you'd be late tonight," she said, relishing the freedom she felt at being able to greet him like this.

He pulled forward and her arms fell away. She thought he'd turn around, but he didn't. "I changed my mind." He tapped the end of his pen against the file in his lap. "After you said you had a dinner appointment, I decided to bring these home. I've got to be in New York next week, so I won't have time to revamp the seminar outline I need for the Denver conference unless I do it now. What time is it?"

Though an uncomfortable knot had just formed in her throat, she managed to sound casual. "Almost ten. When's the Denver conference?"

"A week from Wednesday."

Skirting the sofa, she leaned against its arm and hoped that she had only imagined the distance in his voice. One look at him told her that she hadn't.

The giveaway muscle in his jaw was bunched, and he glanced at her only long enough to give her a strained smile. "How'd your appointment go?"

Wasn't he going to kiss her? Take her in his arms and . . . "Ok, I guess. Did the New York trip just come up?" He hadn't mentioned it before.

"A couple of days ago." Something indefinable flickered through the tension in his features. Then, as if he had been debating his action, he reached up and curled his fingers around the back of her neck. "This is going to take a couple more hours, so you'd better go to bed without me." Pulling her head toward him, he brushed a cool kiss to her lips.

The distress in her eyes was barely masked by her faltering smile. "Don't stay up too late," she cautioned, wondering if that smile looked as mechanical as it felt. Something was wrong, and she didn't think it had anything to do with seminars or conferences. She lifted herself to her feet. "See you in the morning."

"Toni." Kyle's arm shot out, and his hand clamped around her wrist. One quick tug brought her back to the arm of the sofa. A second later, his mouth covered hers.

It was the kiss she had been aching for all day. The tender seduction of her senses that left her head reeling and her body craving more. But she wasn't going to get anything more than that debilitating taste of what only he could give her. A breathless moment later he had let her go.

"Good night, Toni," he said, his tone as remote as the look in his eyes.

She could only nod.

When she glanced back just before she started down the hall, she saw his hand cover his face and his shoulders fall with his heavily expelled breath.

For the first time in four nights, Toni slept in

her own bed. And for the first time, she had come face to face with the wall Kyle had built around his heart.

Kyle stood in front of the night-blackened window in the living room and turned away from the indecision revealed in his reflection.

You taught me almost everything I know. And I wanted you to be the one to teach me how to love.

He wished he'd never asked the question that had prompted those words. But he had been too stunned after discovering that he had taken her virginity to realize how haunting her response would be.

His neat analysis of why Toni had become the woman she had appeared to be had been completely shattered. He had been convinced that she was rebelling against some hidden pain. That she was denying that pain the same way he had. He knew now that he was wrong. Toni only worked as hard as she did because she was the type of person who put everything she had into her efforts. Just as she had given herself so completely to him.

He didn't want to ask her why she had done that. He already suspected the reason. And that reason was something he didn't want to hear.

He wanted her. More than he'd ever wanted any woman in his life. But he was feeling threatened. Not by Toni. By that part of him that had resigned itself to acceptance of what could never be.

That part of him that was again wanting the impossible.

Kyle was gone when Toni awoke the next morning. At first, she wondered if he'd even gone to bed. His rumpled sheets indicated that he had—and that his sleep had been as restless as hers.

All day long she tried to tell herself that there was nothing to worry about. That he'd just needed to be alone to get his work done. Her logical mind wasn't buying that argument and forced her heart to acknowledge another reason.

Kyle ran from commitment like everyone else ran from fire. She didn't think she had said or done anything to make him feel that way, but it was quite possible that he was beginning to feel pressured. That was the last thing she wanted.

She shoved the lasagna Madeline had made last Saturday into the oven. Hunger was one thing she wasn't feeling. She didn't even know if Kyle would be home for dinner. It was just that the routine of preparing a meal gave her something to do besides pace. That's what she'd been doing for the past hour while searching her memory to see if she *had* said something.

She hadn't been able to think of a thing.

"What's the frown for?"

The sound of Kyle's voice sent her heart skidding to a halt. She hadn't heard him come in, and she jerked around so quickly that she nearly knocked the empty salad bowl off the counter.

Kyle grabbed for it and shoved it aside.

"Hey," he chuckled, reaching for her. "I didn't

mean to startle you." He pulled her against his chest and drew his knuckles down her cheek. "Are you ok?"

Her shuddering sigh was nothing more than relief. He was holding her, and the thoughtful scowl on his face was the most wonderful thing she had ever seen.

"Of course I'm ok." Maybe he'd think that the faint tremor in her voice was just the result of their closeness. Or the crazy reaction she always had to the scent of his aftershave as he dropped a quick kiss to her lips.

Kyle looked skeptical. "You sure? You're not usually so jumpy." He drew her fingers away from where they clutched his lapels and pressed them between his. "And your hands are shaking."

"Too much coffee, I guess." A lame reason was better than the real one. After all the thoughts that had been plaguing her, she didn't think it would be wise to tell him that she was almost a basket case over the thought of losing him.

He accepted her response with a knowing grin and stepped back to loosen his tie. "Want some help with dinner?"

Toni shook her head. "It's almost ready. I just have to make a salad. Do you want me to fix you a drink?"

"I'll get it." The tie came off and he started working at the buttons of his shirt. "You remember the TaiCom deal I was telling you about?" he started, heading out of the kitchen to the wet bar. "Well, we had a meeting with the principals of the parent corporation today and . . ." His words were muffled by the wall, but he didn't seem to care as he continued.

Toni sank against the counter and closed her eyes. Kyle was acting like nothing had happened. Not that anything really had, she reminded herself. He just had work to do last night. And she had mentally overreacted.

She couldn't help but wonder if being in love just naturally made a person insecure.

Toni's first fears were resurrected a few hours later. Everything had seemed fine. Almost perfect. They had sat curled up together on the sofa watching a rerun of *Blue Lagoon* on cable. Or at least part of it. Halfway through, Kyle had turned off the set, picked her up and carried her to his bed, saying something about creating their own paradise. Toni never was quite sure what he'd said. And it hadn't mattered. His mouth had mastered hers as completely as he had her body when he pushed her down to the mattress long, interminable seconds later.

Now she lay quietly in the curve of his arm. His heartbeat felt steady—strong and even beneath her hand. She snuggled against him, sated. And waited to feel the languorous contentment that always followed their lovemaking.

That peace eluded her, its lulling effects just out of her reach. Though she couldn't see his face, she knew that he was staring up at the ceiling, his thoughts close, yet very far away.

There had been a conflicting urgency and remoteness in his caresses. A physical elusiveness that matched the same conflict she had sensed in him last night.

Her hair spilled over his chest as she rested her chin in the palm of her hand and studied his shadowed features. She could see very little in the darkness. But then he couldn't see the hesitation in her expression that was missing from her words. "Tell me what's wrong, Kyle."

His response was too quick. "What could possibly be wrong?" He coaxed her head back to his shoulder. "I'm having an affair with a beautiful, intelligent woman who also happens to be a very good friend. What more could I want?"

His response revealed more than she had hoped for. Dismissing the odd pang at the word "affair," she latched onto his last question. She hadn't asked what he wanted; she'd asked what was wrong.

"Only you can answer that," she returned softly. "But you know that you can have anything you want."

Did he realize what she was saying? Short of coming right out and telling him that she loved him, she didn't know how else to put it without making it sound like she was pushing.

"We can't always have what we want, princess," he murmured, brushing a feathery kiss across her forehead. "And sometimes we're better off just accepting what we have and not asking for something that can't be given."

To her, it sounded very much like he was saying that he couldn't give her his love. That's what she wanted. But there was something in his voice that made her wonder if he wasn't trying to tell himself something, too.

Her protective instincts wanted to pull away from him, to guard against some hurt that seemed hanging ready to be felt. The tenacity that had seen her through her seduction wouldn't allow it though. She loved him too much to let an unconfirmed supposition intrude.

Kyle must have anticipated those instincts. His arm, circling her shoulder, and his leg, thrown over hers, had already tensed, and she was encouraged by that possessiveness. There were questions she longed to ask, and his open, if not terribly enlightening, response a few moments ago prompted them.

"What did she do to you?"

"She?"

"Your ex-wife," Toni urged, her voice as quiet as his.

"She didn't do anything."

The slight stiffening of his muscles told her otherwise.

Go slow, she warned herself. "What was her name?"

"Lynn."

"Were you married very long?"

"Four years."

This was a little like pulling eyeteeth, but at least he was answering. "Did you love her?"

There was no mistaking the tension in his body now. But he made no attempt to move away. His hand slid up her arm, and she felt his fingers sifting through the long length of her hair. "Yes, Toni. I loved her. And then I hated her." His chest rose beneath her hand. "And then I didn't feel anything at all."

He'd hated someone he'd loved? The suspicion that had been lurking in her mind ever since Saturday night came into focus. Had he hated

Lynn because she had taken his child from him? "Did you ever have any children?" she ventured cautiously.

He just lay there, stroking her hair. "No," he finally sighed. "We never had any children."

The way those hushed words lingered in the silence bothered Toni, but she wasn't sure why.

"What happened then?"

"She walked out on me."

Though Kyle was providing answers, it was obvious that he wasn't going to offer anything that wasn't specifically called for. Not wanting to risk crossing onto more sensitive ground for fear that he might start withdrawing from her, she made herself settle for what little he'd just told her. What was important now was that he didn't feel pressured by their relationship. Only then could she hope to chip away the barrier that kept the love he had once been able to give locked from her.

He'd said that Lynn had done nothing. Yet, Toni had heard the pain in his voice when he said that she'd walked out on him. Was he afraid of that happening again?

"I won't walk out on you," she promised softly.

His arm tightened around her. "Don't make promises you won't be able to keep, princess," he warned, then silenced her unspoken response with his kiss.

By Saturday morning, Kyle had forced himself to face a few pertinent facts. Telling himself that Toni was content with their affair was nothing but self-serving justification. There had been a quietness about her the past couple of days that had nothing to do with the preoccupation with work she had attributed it to. If she'd been concentrating on work, she would have talked to him about it. They could discuss anything—almost.

There was something he needed to talk to her about now, if he could just find the guts to do it. She had given him the perfect opportunity the other night when she'd asked about Lynn. He had just been too proud to volunteer any information about why his marriage had failed. Now, he almost wished Toni had asked, though at the time, he was grateful that she hadn't.

"You're a damn coward," he muttered at his reflection, then took a too-savage stroke with his razor. That earned his scowling reflection a string of equally savage expletives.

He dabbed at the cut he'd just inflicted on his neck. He was only feeling a little guilty. Not suicidal.

"Are you decent in there?"

Madeline's voice rang out from his bedroom doorway.

Kyle grabbed a towel from the rack behind him. Tucking it around his waist, he turned back to the sink to rinse the streaks of shaving cream from his face. "I'm decent," he called back.

"Just wanted to put the sheets away." Quite unabashed by his near-naked state, she pulled open the linen closet at the far end of the counter. "How was your game today?"

When he'd come home, Madeline had been downstairs. Toni was apparently still at her office. "Fine," he mumbled distractedly, and reached for another towel. "I need you to do me a favor, Madeline. Call the florist and have a dozen roses sent to Toni. Then I want . . ."

"Here, or at her office?"

"Here. This afternoon. Then make a reservation for two at The Wharf for . . ." His brow furrowed as he glanced over at his housekeeper. What was she grinning about? "What time did she say she'd be home?"

"She didn't."

"In that case, you'd better make the reservation for eight o'clock. That should give her time."

Kyle turned from the knowing look that graced Madeline's expression, and she directed her question to his back. "Do you want a message sent with the flowers?" she asked, following him into his room and heading toward the door.

"No. No message."

"What color roses then?"

Kyle pulled a pair of cords from a hanger, the muscle in his jaw jumping as he considered Madeline's question. "White," he said. Hearing the door close, he added quietly, "That's the only color you can give a snow princess."

"He went to work?" Toni wasn't really questioning Madeline, so much as she was trying to comprehend the erratic pattern to Kyle's behavior lately.

"Mmmm," Madeline answered, nodding, and unloaded the sacks of groceries she'd just bought. A suspicious smile lurked in her over-bright eyes. "He said to tell you he'd be back by seven."

Toni frowned at the back of Madeline's plaid shirtwaist. Kyle hadn't said anything about going to the office when they'd had coffee together this morning. And she'd gone to bed without him again last night, leaving him to wrestle with his stack of files. It was a little ironic that, until this week, she'd been the one who brought the work home.

"Does Kyle seem all right to you?" There was no sense trying to sound nonchalant. Though Madeline was the epitome of tact—she had quietly assumed the relationship between Toni and Kyle without ever saying anything about it—she was always willing to offer her opinion.

"He seems just fine." She took a brick of cheese and the milk Toni handed her and wedged them into the refrigerator. "A little moody maybe, but that's to be expected."

Madeline was talking in circles. She had been ever since Toni had come in a few minutes ago. "And just why is that to be expected?" Toni asked with an arching eyebrow.

"It just is. Would you mind putting these up for me? I can't reach the top shelf without a stepstool." Toni took the boxes and saw Madeline glance at the clock as she muttered, "They should have been here by now."

"What should have?"

"Oh, nothing. I was just . . ." The doorbell put an end to Madeline's mumblings. "Why don't you get that, dear? I think it's for you anyway."

Toni couldn't help but think that all the grinning little woman needed was a few feathers between her teeth to look like the cat who'd just caught the canary. Obviously she knew something Toni didn't, and Toni couldn't help but wonder what was going on.

Madeline offered her quite biased opinion a few minutes later.

"It's certainly clear enough to me," she pronounced, beaming as Toni touched one of the delicate white petals nestled among the tiny baby's breath. "A man doesn't send roses and plan a romantic dinner unless he's got something on his mind."

"Maybe that 'something' is his work," Toni countered, still unwilling to believe what Madeline was saying—yet, wanting desperately to believe it. "Every night this week he's . . ."

Madeline's interruption was gentle. "I'm sure he's thinking about that, too. Wouldn't it make sense to get everything in order before you took time off for a honeymoon? And besides," she continued, patting Toni's hand, "you don't keep house for a person for over four years without learning something about him. He's ready to settle down, and the minute I saw you two together, I knew you'd be the one who could make him do it. You're nothing like the other . . ." She cleared her throat and hastily gathered up the box of roses to put them into a vase.

Madeline hadn't needed to continue. Toni could well imagine the number of women she had encountered here on Saturday mornings.

"Well, anyway," she continued, "I couldn't be more pleased for either of you. Do you want me to press out the dress you'll be wearing tonight? I'll be leaving in a while, but I'd be happy to do it before I go."

Toni's dress hadn't needed pressing. The soft black jersey clung smoothly to her willowy figure, its simplicity an appropriate counterpoint for the single pearl lying at the base of her throat and the stud pearl earrings she wore. Her hair had been worked into a flattering Gibson, and the candlelight playing across her fragile features captured the warmth hidden beneath her urbane polish, the warmth that was shining in her compelling aquamarine eyes and her softly curved mouth.

It had been over an hour since Kyle had tasted those sweet, inviting lips, felt the promise of surrender in her body as it had flowed against his. And ever since then, he'd been asking himself what kind of idiot would willingly hasten the loss of his lover and best friend.

He reached for his wine and watched Toni lean back for the waiter to remove her plate. She had barely touched her scampi. It was no wonder she was so thin.

"I thought you said the shrimp was good," he said, baiting her with his bland tone.

Surprisingly, she didn't comment on his own lack of appetite. "It was." She glanced out the window. "There was just too much of it."

Outside the huge window they sat beside, she could see a misty fog encroaching upon the sound. The stars were hidden, but the lights from the restaurant cast elongated shimmers across the dark waters lapping against the wooden pilings. Toni barely noticed. She wasn't paying any more attention to the peaceful scenery than she was to the tinkle of crystal and silver punctuating the hushed conversations taking place around them. She was too busy wishing that Madeline had just kept her opinions to herself.

Ever since she had mentioned marriage, Toni had been forced to acknowledge the little voice she had tried to silence. She wasn't cut out to settle for nothing more than an affair, and it was apparent enough that marriage was the furthest thing from Kyle's mind. So far all they'd talked about was the upcoming mayoral election and how torn up the streets were now that the city was finally putting in new sewers. Hardly topics preparatory to a proposal.

"Why do you wear that?"

Kyle's quiet question pulled her from her thoughts, and she slanted him a puzzled glance.

He nodded toward her hand. It was at her throat. "The necklace," he prompted. "Why do you always wear it?"

"Oh, I . . ." She withdrew her fingers from the pearl she'd been toying with and smiled faintly. "I bought it a long time ago . . . when I was working for you. You had just given me an hour-long lecture on how *not* to work the options board and had told me that I'd be well advised to remember what you'd said." Her lips curved more generously as she recalled the names she'd silently called him that day. "Arrogant, insufferable jerk" being the kindest. "I wear it to remind me not to forget those pearls of wisdom."

He caught a flash of her old, mischievous smile, then watched her grow pensive again.

You taught me almost everything I know. And I wanted you to be the one to teach me how to love.

Kyle let out a deep breath, wishing he could as easily expel the words that had become a tormenting litany. "I guess I was pretty hard on you," he admitted, turning a mental change of subject. "But you've got to admit that you gave as good as you got after a while."

"Self-defense," she returned. "It was either fight back or join the ranks of all the other people trembling in your wake."

"You saying that I was hard to work for?"

"I'm saying that you were almost *impossible* to work for."

He leaned forward, crossing his arms on the table as Toni had just done. "But not impossible to live with."

The animation that had slipped into Toni's eyes vanished abruptly. Kyle's question wasn't a casual one. And she could only hope where it might lead.

"You're very easy to live with," she replied softly.

A surge of anticipation gripped her as he reached over and curled her fingers through his.

"We're good together, princess." He stroked her palm with his thumb, caressed her face with his eyes. "What we've got is something special. And I don't want to lose you."

Though she held his intent gray eyes steadily, mentally she closed her own and held her breath.

"I want you to live with me," he continued, feeling her fingers tighten around his. A smile touched his lips. "And you don't need to tell me that you already are. What I want is for you to forget about finding a place of your own. Have all the stuff you've got in storage back in New York sent to the house. There's plenty of room for it and we could use . . ."

The pressure of her fingers relaxed, making their trembling evident. "What . . . what are you asking?" she interrupted, her eyes cautiously searching.

His voice was deep and even. "That you stay with me. I need you, Toni."

Need. Not love. Stay. Not marry. "And then what?" The tremor in her hand was threatening to become apparent in her voice.

Kyle looked down at the table, his eyes shuttered from her by the heavy bank of his black lashes. He avoided her question. "We have everything we need already."

Toni slowly pulled her hand away, flinching inwardly when she saw his jaw tense. His tacit words were telling her what she had known all along. That no matter how much she loved him, how patiently she tried to understand him, that he was incapable of real commitment. He wanted only what they had now, and nothing more. Madeline had been wrong. So very wrong.

The dull heaviness centering in her chest made it difficult to speak, but she managed. "Maybe I don't have everything I need, Kyle."

"What more is there?"

If it hadn't been for the slightly defensive edge in his tone, Toni would have sworn that he honestly didn't know.

They had been through this before. But this wasn't that long-ago exchange of attitudes. It was two people finally coming to grips with some very basic differences. "For you?" she questioned quietly. "I really don't know. But for me, there's love and commitment and . . ."

"Marriage?" he said, completing her sentence. He was staring down at the table, twisting the edge of his napkin.

Toni thought it odd that he hadn't choked on the word. "Yes," she admitted. "Marriage."

The word seemed to hang in the heavy silence, intensifying the shattering effect of his quiet inspection. She was falling apart inside, and tenaciously holding on to the last vestiges of hope that the uncertainty in his eyes was giving her.

That hope died the instant she saw uncertainty being replaced with defense.

"I'm not going to ask you to live with any illusions, Toni. We've been friends too long for that. You and I can never have anything different from what we have now. As far as I'm concerned, the only reason to get married is to have children. And since I don't want them, I can't see where a piece of paper is necessary."

That's not what he'd meant to say at all. But his pride had gotten in the way again.

He must have realized that his voice, if not his words, had drawn the attention of the people behind them. Both his tone and his expression grew softer. "Right now, we've got more going for us than most couples I know, and I can't see any reason for us to get married. It wouldn't change how we feel, or what we do. And I'm willing to live with what we've got if you are."

His eyes darted from her too-quiet expression to the woman who was openly watching them now. "Let's get out of here," he sighed, tossing a handful of bills on the table. "This isn't any place to discuss this."

No reason to get married . . . don't want children . . . live with what we've got. Those fragmented phrases ripped through her heart.

Her nerveless fingers gripped the table as she pushed herself away. "I can't see where there's anything left to discuss, Kyle." She couldn't look at him. "You've made your point."

Chapter Eight

Toni knew that Kyle had been priming himself for an argument ever since they'd left the restaurant. All the signs were there—the formidable clenching of his jaw, the rigid set of his broad shoulders, a tightly wound spring just waiting for the slightest pressure to send it uncoiling.

Toni said nothing, preferring the forbidding stillness to engaging in what could only become a heated verbal battle. She wasn't about to plead her case. She'd swallowed enough of her pride when she'd set out to seduce him—and look where that had gotten her.

The oppressive silence that had filled the car during their drive home accompanied them into the house. Toni left Kyle in the entry and headed for her room, praying that she could hang on to the strange calm mercifully numbing her senses until . . . until what?

Until you can get out of here, she answered herself, haphazardly tossing the contents of her drawers into the suitcases she'd just pulled from her closet. Then you can go somewhere and quietly fall to pieces.

Kyle would never change. So what point was there in beating her head against a brick wall? She'd only be compromising herself if she stayed. Kyle had said that he didn't want to get married because he didn't want children. That was nothing but an excuse. She'd seen how he enjoyed playing with Todd's boys. The wistfulness in his eyes when he talked about Jana's little girl. Maybe he meant that he didn't want her to have his children.

The pain in her heart was beginning to have disastrous effects on her thinking processes. Right now, she'd be better off not to think at all.

She pulled an armload of suits from the rack and glanced up just in time to see Kyle pushing open the door.

He had taken off his shirt and tie. Without those trappings of civility, the irritation she had sensed in him seemed more pronounced, his lean, male form more threatening somehow.

That same threat was in his voice. "What do you think you're doing?"

"I don't think I'm doing anything," she returned, amazed at how calm she sounded. "What I *am* doing is packing."

"You're not planning on going anywhere tonight, are you? It's almost eleven, for God's sake!"

She didn't really know what she was planning. She was on auto-pilot. The same numbness that controlled her features was also in charge of her actions.

Closing the latch on the suitcase she had just filled, she pulled the other one toward her. She sounded every bit as reasonable as Kyle did angry. "If you'll excuse the use of a worn-out old adage, it's better late than never. You know something, Kyle?" She didn't look at him, or wait for a response. "I never realized how much I procrastinate. I'm always telling myself that I'm too busy, or too preoccupied, or too tired to do some of the things I know I should do. I kept promising myself that I'd hire an assistant. That I'd start getting some exercise. That I'd find a place to live." A tight little laugh slid past the constriction in her throat. "The only reason I bought a car when I did was because I didn't have any other choice. You literally took me by the hand and made me do it." She headed back to the closet. "I guess it's kind of like now. I don't have any choice. There's no sense waiting for things to change, because they're not going to."

"It's not like you to run away from something."

"I'm not running away." She caught a glimpse of him when she turned around. His arms were folded across his chest and his challenging frame filled the doorway. "Quite the opposite, actually. I'm just facing facts."

"And what are those facts?" he demanded.

The methodical motions of packing reinforced

her almost-methodical thoughts. "That I've been deceiving myself . . . and you."

"Me?"

Her back was to him, so she didn't see the disquiet in his narrowed eyes. "Both of us," she told him softly.

"How did you deceive me?"

Was that anger or hurt she detected in his question? She couldn't tell. And she didn't trust herself to look at him to find out. "By letting you think that I'm something I'm not. That I'd be willing to settle for a relationship that won't ever lead anywhere. I think I was trying to convince myself of that same thing for the past couple of weeks. Even though I kept hoping that my . . . that how I felt about you would eventually make you feel the same way, I guess I always knew that I already had all I was going to get." She turned toward him, her eyes skimming his powerful chest, then lowering to the floor. "You either won't . . . or can't . . . give me what I need."

Her last words seemed to take a second to sink in and his silence drew her eyes to his. For one heart-stopping moment, she saw the anguish in his expression. But it remained only long enough for him to drag his fingers through his hair.

"I don't think we should talk about this right now," he stated flatly. "I don't want you to leave, but I think we're both too upset to discuss this rationally. One of us is going to wind up saying something not meant, so let's talk about it in the morning."

Toni thought she was being quite rational. "I'm not upset, Kyle." Indeed, she had never felt more . . . detached. "And I won't be here in the morning."

Pulling on the camel's hair coat she'd thrown across the dresser, she picked up her suitcases and started for the door. "I can't walk through you," she sighed. "So would you please get out of the way?"

It had been a mistake to get so close to him. Before she could widen the distance, his hands had curved over her shoulders, his thumbs running too lightly along the side of her neck. He nodded toward the suitcases.

"Put them down, Toni."

The feel of his hands and the intensity in his expression removed every trace of her benumbed state. If he kissed her, held her, she wouldn't stand a chance. His head was inching lower.

She couldn't let him do this. Without that deceptive numbness, she could feel only the hurt. And the screaming need of her heart for him to hold her and make that hurt go away.

Her only defense against him now was to allow anger to mask that pain. "Stop being childish," she said, berating him. "And let go of me."

She had just made mistake number two.

"Childish?" The word seemed to explode through the room. Kyle jerked his hands back, his own anger unleashed by her accusation. "To quote another old adage, isn't that a little like the pot calling the kettle black? If either one of us is being juvenile, it's most definitely you!

You're still clinging to a bunch of outdated ideas about rose-covered cottages and living happily ever after. Well, I've got news for you, princess." The way he drew out that once-teasing endearment made it sound very belittling. "Things like that only happen in fairy tales. If you can't handle a mature relationship without deluding yourself about . . ."

"Don't talk to me about not being mature," she snapped. "A mature person wouldn't be afraid to commit himself. And that's what you're afraid of, isn't it? You just don't have the guts to take a chance!"

His eyes glinted dangerously. "You don't know what you're talking about. And if you had any guts, you'd stay."

He was the one who didn't know what he was saying. It was taking far more courage to leave than it would to stay and live with the man she loved so desperately. But she had to be able to live with herself, too.

Kyle had moved from the door. Swallowing back the retort burning on her lips, she swept out into the hallway. She didn't even notice the cumbersome weight of her luggage. For all the attention she was paying to those heavy cases, they might as well have been packed with feathers.

"Toni! Come back here! You aren't going to walk out in the middle of this!"

It was hardly the middle of anything.

She had just opened the front door when Kyle came bursting into the entryway.

She nudged the door open further. They were doing just what Kyle had said he'd wanted to avoid—saying things they knew they'd both regret. It was up to her to make sure things didn't get worse.

"I can't stay, Kyle." There was a plea for understanding in her unsteady glance. "I can't just live with you. And I think enough has been said already."

She hurried out, but not before she caught a glimpse of the white roses sitting on the coffee table. Her heart wrenched painfully. It seemed like a century ago since she'd stood in that same entry, thanking him for those twelve perfect roses with her loving kiss.

Right on the heels of that unwanted thought came the ones she'd been trying to avoid.

Kyle cared about her. She knew that. But only enough to ask her to share his bed. He didn't care enough to marry her.

And right on the heels of that came Kyle.

He stood at the edge of the flagstone walkway, his rigid stance illuminated by the porch light. There was a look of resignation shadowing his features, and he made no attempt to move toward her car.

Apparently he didn't even care enough to try to keep her from going.

Toni fought back another surge of anguish, telling herself to be reasonable. She didn't want him to stop her.

"If I've left anything here"—she shoved her luggage into her car, praying that the moisture she could feel brimming in her eyes was something, anything, other than tears. Where was all that sophistication she'd prided herself on?— "send whatever it is to my office. The box in the bottom of the closet belongs to Madeline. I'd appreciate it if you'd give it to her." She couldn't quite bring herself to have Kyle add her thanks.

"Where will you be staying?"

She didn't miss the concern in his voice, or the pain revealed in his tense features. "Greg will know," she choked, more to herself than to Kyle. Greg had all those rental houses she'd found for him. Maybe he'd let her rent one.

She closed herself inside the car, shutting Kyle out completely.

Toni hadn't realized the devastating impact of her response. All she knew when she dared one last glance toward the house was that she'd never forget the dejection in Kyle's stance, or the contradicting rage darkening his beautiful face.

Kyle stood at the edge of the walkway for several long minutes after Toni had pulled out of the drive. There had been no point in trying to stop her. He had nothing more to offer than what he already had. He tried to tell himself that he should just be thankful that he hadn't been forced to tell her why. It didn't matter now anyway.

That night, Kyle did something he hadn't done in years. He went back into the house and got himself rip-roaring drunk.

Toni did something she hadn't allowed herself to do in years either. After reaching the bottom of the hill, she pulled the car off the road, folded her arms over the steering wheel, and cried.

"How's the house?"

Toni closed the file she and Greg had been

discussing over lunch and reached for her coffee. Now that their business was concluded, his question seemed perfectly logical.

"It's just fine," she returned, thinking about the small one-bedroom house she was now living in. It was such a drastic change from . . . "I like it." She didn't want to think about the spacious home she'd left over two weeks ago.

"And how about you?" Greg's blond head dipped slightly, seeking her lowered eyes. "How's Toni?"

That question, unfortunately, was perfectly logical, too. When she'd met Greg after spending a long, tear-filled night at a hotel following her argument with Kyle, she'd looked more than a little haggard. She hadn't said why she'd needed a place in such a hurry, and Greg hadn't asked. "I guess I'm fine, too."

She hoped she sounded convincing.

Apparently she didn't. Greg smiled sympathetically. "If you need someone to talk to, we doctors are known to be very good listeners."

She didn't want to talk. Not about Kyle anyway. So a change of subject was called for. Greg liked to talk about himself and that seemed like a safe direction to head in. "So, you're a doctor now? A minute ago you were a big business tycoon. I assume you're also half tennis pro, since you said you aced your opponent this morning." They were having lunch at his club, and he was still wearing his tennis whites. "What else are you on your day off?"

Toni was surprised when he didn't go for the bait and he turned the topic right back around. "A friend. Or maybe I should say, a friendly

doctor." He watched her place her cup back on
her saucer and finger the pearl lying against her
blue silk blouse. "Your hands are shaking. You
ordered cream soup . . . which you didn't eat
because you kept your arms crossed over your
stomach like someone would who was trying to
ease acidic discomfort. I would also guess that
you're suffering from insomnia by the edema
and"—he caught himself, opting for civilian
terms rather than medical ones—"by the puffi-
ness and dark circles under your eyes. I don't
want you to think I'm trying to drum up business," he continued with a negative movement
of his head. "Stress isn't my field anyway. But I
do recognize the symptoms."

She tried to laugh, something that had seemed
a little difficult to do lately. "That bad, huh?"

He nodded gravely. "Sometimes it helps to
talk when something's bothering you. I don't
want to pry, but if you think it would help to get
it off your chest, just let me know." He softened
his professionalism with a dentist-perfect grin.
"I owe you for all that free investment advice
you gave me."

Only part of it had been free. He'd been
charged a walloping fee for most of her services.

Greg may have been one of the most conceited
men she'd ever known—not without some justification, she'd finally concluded—but he was a
doctor. And, in a way, they were friends.

She needn't have bothered with that rationalization. Before she knew it, Greg had drawn her
out. She didn't have to say much for him to get a
pretty clear picture of what had happened. But
the only advice he offered was to start getting

some exercise, ease up on the coffee, and call him if that didn't make it easier to sleep. He wouldn't prescribe sleeping pills himself—not that she wanted any—but he said he'd have one of his colleagues check her out and give her some if that doctor thought they were necessary. Definitely professional.

When Toni returned to her office that afternoon, she felt better than she had in days. Talking had helped. The dull void in her chest was still there, but she was more determined than ever to stop torturing herself with thoughts of dreams that could never be fulfilled. She'd gotten over Kyle once before—when she'd moved to New York. Not that that could really compare to what was happening now. Then, she had only fantasies. Now, she had to contend with realities. Knowing what it felt like to be held by him, to make love with him, made dealing with this loss so much more difficult. Even harder to cope with was the fact that she'd lost her best friend.

Another week passed. Toni dutifully followed Greg's advice by jogging in the park by her house whenever she could—and trying to cut down on her caffeine consumption. Some things were easier than others. She felt like she was finally making progress though. She didn't even think about Kyle anymore—anymore than every other hour anyway. Negligible as it seemed, that *was* an improvement.

Yes. She smiled to herself, pulling off her perspiration-damp sweatsuit and stepping into the shower. She'd finally hired that assistant she'd promised herself and had actually arrived home at four o'clock two days in a row. *I'm going to be just fine.*

At least that's what she thought until the phone calls started.

She had been out the first time Kyle called. Knowing that just the sound of his voice might undo her completely, she very carefully tore up the pink message slip into about twenty little pieces and dropped them into her wastebasket. The second time he called, Toni was in.

Instead of taking the call, she told her secretary to tell him she was on her way out. Then, to save her secretary the embarrassment of telling an outright lie, she backed up her words by going to the ladies' room.

The third call came two days later. It was from Madeline.

"How are you, dear?" There was a wealth of genuine concern in Madeline's question.

Toni's grip tightened on the receiver. It felt like an entire butterfly collection had just been unleashed in her stomach.

Telling herself that just because Madeline worked for Kyle was no reason to come unglued, she managed an easy reply. "I'm just fine. And how are you doing? How's your back?" She was thinking of all the times she'd seen Madeline frowning while she worked her weathered hands over her stiff shoulders.

"Well, I'm . . . that is . . ."

A little warning bell went off in Toni's head. She didn't think that Madeline's hesitation was because she was pondering the state of her health. Certainly she must know how she was feeling.

"Yes, Madeline?" Toni prompted, keeping the suspicion from her tone. Had Kyle put her up to this call?

"Oh, I'm just as good as ever . . . and I . . . well, I didn't want to bother you at work. I mean, I know how busy you are, and I didn't have your phone number to call you . . . to call you at home. . . ." She definitely sounded nervous. And that didn't sound like Madeline. ". . . If it's not convenient for you right now . . ."

"I'm not busy." That was a lie, but a harmless one. Leaning back in her chair, Toni stared out the window—it was raining again—and waited for a more fluid string of words.

She finally heard them.

"Well," Madeline began again. "You left a few things here. Some underthings. They were in the laundry. I didn't think you'd want them sent to your office like Kyle said to do. So, if you'll give me your new address . . ."

Her address. So that was it. Her secretary had said that a man had called yesterday wanting to verify her new residence. When she'd asked him to give her the address he had so she could confirm it, he'd hung up.

Toni had suspected who that "man" might have been. Now she was sure of it. If she still couldn't trust herself to talk to Kyle on the phone, she certainly wouldn't be able to handle it if he showed up at her door.

"Why don't you take the things home with you?" Toni suggested. "I'd love to see you, and maybe we could visit for a while." Then, not wanting to have it work out that Kyle could just happen to be there, she quickly added, "I'm not sure when I could stop by, but we could work something out later."

Toni could almost see the defeat that must have been revealed in Madeline's face. It was sure evident in her voice. "Oh," she sighed. "I guess that would be all right. Do you still have my phone number?"

"Yes." Toni smiled. "I do. And, Madeline, you can tell that boss of yours that he's got a very loyal housekeeper. I just hope he appreciates you." Kyle wouldn't like that at all.

The chuckle that met Toni's ear held relief. "I told him I didn't think I could pull it off. But you know how insistent he can be." Madeline's tone grew serious. "He's trying so hard to pretend that he doesn't miss you. Ever since he's been back in town, he's seemed so miserable."

She didn't need to hear things like this. But that didn't stop her from listening to what was being offered. Toni didn't want Kyle to be miserable. Any more than she wanted to be that way herself. She just wanted to forget. . . .

The kindly woman's voice intruded. "You did know that he'd been gone, didn't you?"

Toni had known. He'd been in Denver and then in New York. She'd felt safe during those weeks, knowing that he was away, terribly threatened now that he had returned.

"Yes," she answered quietly. "And thanks for calling, Madeline."

With a deliberately controlled effort, she hung

up and turned back to her work. It was harder than ever to concentrate now.

That phone call had been disturbing enough. But Toni didn't suffer any major setbacks until the next day.

She was sitting at her desk straightening the stacks of files and computer printouts threatening to overtake it before her last appointment showed up. Her meeting was with a prospective new client. A Mr. Dentworth who, her secretary had told her, had been referred by Dr. Greg Nichols.

Her task somewhat accomplished, she smoothed the front of her mauve and gray herringbone skirt, flicked a speck of lint from the lapel of her dark gray jacket and touched her fingers to the high jabot of her pearl gray blouse to make sure the knot was straight. Her hair, in its usual chignon, gleamed with polished highlights, and her regime of exercise had given a healthy glow to a complexion that had been verging toward pale. She knew she would present a picture of absolute professionalism and confidence. It was important to do that, especially with a new client. After all, the man was going to trust her with something that meant a lot to him. His money.

The expected knock came from the other side of her door.

Pushing the one remaining file to the side, she prepared a businesslike smile of greeting. "Come in," she answered crisply, and stood up.

She sat right back down.

A sound that was somewhere between a gasp

and a moan preceded words that could only be described as strangled. "What are you doing here?"

Kyle closed the door, shutting out the noise of the telephones ringing in the large outer office so he could be heard. "I have an appointment."

His voice exuded all the self-assurance of his bearing. Everything, from the almost arrogant tilt of his head to the flawless cut of the pin-striped suit, emphasizing the muscular frame beneath it, indicated a man very much in control of himself, and the situation.

Toni wasn't feeling anywhere near that confident.

She did her best to pretend otherwise, though, as he moved toward her desk.

"You obviously used a phony name to get in here," she accused, hiding the defensiveness in her tone with what she hoped was calm indifference. Indifference? She could never feel that way toward him. He looked wonderful. And, God, how she'd missed him! "And I don't appreciate it."

There was a trace of his old, teasing smile threatening at the corners of his cool gray eyes. "It's not a phony name," he replied, coming around the corner of her desk. He leaned against it, crossing his legs at the ankles and leaning back slightly on his palms. "It's my mother's."

She couldn't remember if she'd ever known that. Not that it mattered. What mattered was that in one lousy second, he'd managed to undo what had taken her weeks to accomplish. Not one of those silent, determined peptalks about how she was finally getting over him held a modicum of conviction.

"I'm sure you didn't come here to discuss your mother." She slanted him an exacting glance. "And any other subject you had in mind would be a waste of time. Since I obviously don't have an appointment right now, you'll excuse me while I get on with something else." With a defiance she didn't feel, she reached for the file he was nearly sitting on.

His hand came down on top of hers, his touch so hot that it felt like her hand was melting into the wood beneath it. He kept it there, pressing his down more firmly when she tried to pull away.

"You have an appointment with me," he responded with equanimity. "And your secretary said you don't have any others for the rest of the day."

"Why would she tell you that?" She was trying not to think about the heat of his hand, the determination in his eyes, and her thought was verbalized before she realized it.

"Because I asked her."

Kyle was used to getting his way. In fact, he insisted on it. His response was typical of that expectation.

Seeing the consternation flick through her guarded blue eyes, he added, "Don't worry. She was quite protective of you. She only told me after I mentioned that we might have to go look at a piece of property after our meeting and I asked if you'd be available."

A moment ago, her composure had been hanging by a thread. Now it was being reinforced by a surge of welcomed anger. With one swift movement, she freed her hand and rolled her chair back. Then, skirting the opposite side of her desk, she turned sharply to face him.

"Listen, Donovan," she said, seething quietly. "I don't know what you want. And I don't care to know. But I won't have you manipulating my staff with lies. You've been here long enough already and I want you to leave. Now!"

Kyle didn't look the least bit affected by either her proclamation, or the challenge in her stance.

Taking his time, he pushed himself from the desk and absently adjusted the crisp white cuff of his shirt to the proper half-inch below his dark jacket sleeve as he followed the path she had just taken.

If he was leaving, he was going the wrong way.

Toni had taken a defensive step back when he stopped in front of her—only to find further progress impeded by one of the white leather guest chairs. She couldn't move to the side either. The bookcase was there.

"I haven't told any lies," he said calmly. "There is a piece of property. I want to take you there."

His eyes held her, pinning her to her spot on the green carpet so effectively that she couldn't have moved if she'd wanted to. And she did want to. Otherwise, she might find herself giving in to the urge to touch the face that still haunted her dreams. He was so close that she could smell the faint, spicy scent of his cologne, and that brought a rush of response shuddering through the longing in her body.

"What property?" she managed, fighting an odd ambivalence that wanted nothing more than to go with him. Nothing less than for him to go away.

He curved his fingers over her shoulders, one hand moving up to lay against the side of her neck. He must have felt her stiffen, because the weight of his hands increased as he slid his thumb along the line of her jaw. "My house." His thumb stroked her bottom lip. "I want you to come home."

Home. He made it sound like she belonged there.

She closed her eyes and tried to turn her head away when a painful whimper snagged in her throat.

Kyle caught that anguished lament with his kiss.

Toni knew she should pull back, do something to protect herself from what could only lead to more pain. His arms were tightening around her back, pressing her slender curves to the familiar contours of his harder ones, and his lips were softly demanding. She couldn't seem to do a thing to stop him.

Her heart and her mind were locked in a battle her body ignored. Parting her lips beneath his gentle insistence, she arched against him.

"I knew it," he breathed in quiet triumph. "I knew you wouldn't be able to forget." He captured her mouth again, claiming what was so undeniably his.

Toni's mind refused to function. She couldn't think of all the reasons why he was so wrong for her when all she wanted to do was lose herself in his solid strength. She loved him. She always had. And probably, God help her, always would.

The pressure of his arms relaxed, and she felt the smooth-rough touch of his fingers tilting her chin up when he raised his head to look down at her. His other arm held her firmly, offering the support her weakened legs could not.

His eyes searched her face, narrowing at the confusion of emotions revealed there. She was rapidly replacing desire and need—and something that looked suspiciously like the love he had seen there so often before—with a determined mask of resolve.

He couldn't let that happen.

"I've missed you, princess." His tone was soothing, and he trailed his fingers down her throat to slide them beneath her jacket. Her heart felt like it was doing double-time. So did his. "I miss waking up next to you in the morning. Feeling your breasts grow hard in my hands."

To emphasize his disconcerting words, his hand folded over one expectedly taut breast. Even through her blouse, he could feel her responding to his touch. He pulled her closer to prevent her from moving. "I miss talking with you," he continued, watching the struggle going on in her mind reveal itself in her eyes. "And all you have to do is tell me that you don't love me, and I'll leave you alone."

In less than a second, he felt her go limp, then

absolutely rigid. Knowing that he had just played his trump card, he slowly pulled back and watched her grab for the arm of the chair.

He'd negotiated some pretty risky deals in his time, but never had any of them come close to meaning what this one did.

Toni drew a steadying breath. Then, another. She was too stunned to speak. Not that her mind was providing anything to say at the moment.

Her hesitation, and the fact that he could read nothing in her expression other than shock, forced Kyle to prompt a response.

"Look at me, Toni. Look at me and tell me that you don't love me." He knew how arrogant that must sound. But that arrogance had always allowed him to get what he wanted in the past. Almost everything he wanted anyway. "Then, I want you to tell me that you really don't want to live with me."

Live with me. Not "marry me."

"Damn you, Donovan." She whirled toward him, her mind functioning at full capacity now. "Damn you!"

His surprise at her vehemence vanished with the slow blink of his lashes. "That's not an answer," he reminded evenly.

"Well, you're not going to get one!" As much as she wanted to deny her feelings, she simply couldn't. But there was no way he was going to walk out the door with her pride in his pocket. "You're willing to take, but you're not willing to give anything back! No, Kyle, I don't want to live with you!"

The complacency in his expression faltered.

In his cool gray eyes, she could see a question forming.

"The reason you don't want to live with me wouldn't be because you're living with Greg, would it?"

Kyle hadn't even thought of that possibility until now. Sure, she'd run to Greg when she'd left Kyle, but . . . He left his thought unfinished when he saw the sparks of fury forming in her eyes. Toni wasn't that kind of a woman, and he was already delivering a scathing recrimination to himself for asking such a stupid question when he heard her barely controlled response.

"Where I'm living is none of your business!" She couldn't quite believe that this was happening. How could two people who had shared so much turn on each other like this? "Now, get out of here before I . . ."

She was saved the trouble of coming up with a viable threat when her door creaked open. A pair of bespectacled eyes darted from an obviously agitated Toni to a very attractive and quite composed Kyle.

"I don't mean to interrupt, but is everything all right in here?" Theresa, Toni's secretary, looked a little uncomfortable as she glanced back at her boss.

Apparently Toni's voice had been heard in the outer office. Toni didn't know whether to shrug it off or feel mortified. She never lost her temper —with anyone but Kyle.

"Everything will be fine in a minute." Her assurance was delivered in a tone considerably more subdued than it had been seconds before. "Mr. Donovan was just leaving."

"Donovan? I thought he said his name was Dentworth."

"His name's Donovan." Toni focused firmly on Kyle's maddeningly nonplused expression, not taking her eyes from his, even though her words were for her secretary. "And if you ever see him in this office again, call security."

Theresa showed an admirable amount of professional aplomb by acknowledging Toni with a calm, "Yes, ma'am," and swinging the door wide. She stood back, waiting for the about-to-be-evicted Mr. Donovan to pass.

Kyle ignored the woman long enough to deliver one parting remark. He sounded just as unperturbed as he looked. "You still haven't denied it, Ms. Collins. And I suggest you remember what I said. I've offered you a deal and you'd be well advised to consider it."

With that, he turned one of his debilitatingly sexy grins on her secretary. Touching his finger to the dark hair falling casually over his forehead, he gave a wide-eyed Theresa a smart little salute and walked out the door.

Toni sank into the chair in front of her desk. She was shaking—with rage, she told herself. Kyle had just made it sound like they'd been having a business discussion! And Theresa probably thought that her boss had just gone off the deep end by yelling at a client!

"Are you ok, Toni?"

Theresa was still hovering in the doorway, no doubt being eaten alive with curiosity. The only thing Toni could think to say that would keep office tongues from wagging also happened to be the truth. "He works for the competition,

Theresa," she said, smoothing her skirt as she stood. "And you know how dirty the competition can play. Would you bring me a cup of coffee . . . and the Ellsworth portfolio?"

And that, she hoped, was the end of that.

It wasn't the end of anything though. And Toni knew it.

Kyle had said he'd leave her alone—if she denied that she loved him. Well, she hadn't denied it, and he wasn't leaving her alone.

The first perfect white rose was delivered by Theresa at ten o'clock the next morning. Toni waited until her secretary had discreetly departed before opening the florist's card that had come with it. The challenging message was short, and definitely to the point. *Deny it.*

The card wasn't signed. But, then, it didn't have to be.

The second rose, white and perfect like the first one, was waiting for her when she returned from lunch. This time all the card said was, *Don't deny it.*

Why was he doing this to her?

Toni's elbows were propped up on her desk, and she let the card slip from her fingers to bury her face in her hands. Kyle would never understand. She could beg him, plead with him, try to make him see that she had to have the commitment of his love and the promise of stability. She couldn't live with him otherwise. But Kyle would never understand why she needed those things. She wasn't so sure she understood it herself. It was just some basic conviction that seemed pointless to question. Even if she went to him on his terms, her love alone wouldn't be enough to hold them together forever.

Her head hurt. The weight of the heavy coil piled on top of it wasn't helping either. She tucked a loosened strand back up into the side, and her hand fell limply to the desk.

Kyle liked her hair. So many times she'd watched the fascination in his eyes when he'd slowly remove the pins and tumble the long, pale tresses through his fingers. So many times he had taken that shimmering veil and buried his face in . . .

Pushing herself from the desk, she stood up and leaned against it. She'd been thinking about getting her hair cut to a more manageable length for quite a while. It took forever to wash and dry it. One of these days, she'd . . .

That unfinished thought joined the other.

One of these days nothing, she reprimanded herself, and turned to pick up her phone. *You've been getting better at not putting things off, and you're not going to start backsliding now.*

Jana would probably know of a good hair-dresser, and Toni dialed the number automatically. There was no reason to look it up. It had been her own work number for a while—and was still Kyle's.

She didn't bother to wonder if it had been her thoughts of him, or the headache, that prompted her decision to make and keep the appointment she made for the following Tuesday.

"Are you sure you wanted to do that?" Two minutes ago, Jana had been full of ego-boosting compliments. Now, she wasn't bothering to hide her skepticism while she eyed Toni's shoulder-length hair. "It takes so long to grow out, and it did look awfully nice when you wore it up."

"I can still wear it up," Toni defended lightly. "See?"

She swept her hand up the back of her neck to show Jana that she wouldn't have any trouble making a chignon out of it if she wanted.

Jana shrugged with a smile. "I suppose it probably doesn't feel anywhere near as heavy," she conceded, watching Toni give her head a quick shake and the curve of swingy, light blond hair fall back to her shoulders. "And it does make you look . . . well, softer, I think."

Toni's already husky voice lowered several notches. "Less like the tyrant of Wall Street?"

"How about more like a college sophomore." Jana grinned at Toni's moan and ducked behind her menu.

Jana had insisted that Toni meet her at a nearby steakhouse after her hair appointment, and Toni was glad that she had. For once, she wasn't thinking about Kyle. Jana was good company—even if she did seem a little preoccupied. Toni couldn't help but notice that the petite brunette had developed quite a fixation with her watch, and the front door of the restaurant.

"I think I'd like another drink before we order." Jana folded her menu and signaled their waitress. "How about it?"

Toni was game. "Why not?"

Their second round of drinks was delivered and Jana was halfway through an amusing discourse on the unpredictable toilet habits of three-year olds when Toni glanced up to see

Todd talking with the young girl who had seated them. The girl was nodding toward their table.

She knew that Jana and Todd had gone out a couple of times, strictly on a casual basis—according to Jana, Todd had his eye on the new file girl Kyle had just hired—and she now knew why Jana had been watching the door.

"Todd's here." Toni smiled and watched Jana's head jerk sideways then quickly back.

Jana had a very strange look on her face. And when Toni looked back over at Todd, she knew why.

Kyle was with him.

"Toni, please," Jana said, seeing the look in Toni's eyes that clearly spelled "traitor." "I told Todd I couldn't go out with him tonight because I was having dinner with you. He mentioned it to Kyle, and . . ."

"Hi, ladies." Todd's greeting lacked a little of his typical effusiveness as he slid into the booth next to Jana. "We got tied up in . . ." He cut off his explanation about why they were late when he looked over at Toni. "Hey! I like your hair!"

Kyle didn't. That was apparent enough by the scowl he was directing at Toni's head. He must have realized that his opinion wouldn't help his position any because he immediately softened his expression. "You don't mind if we crash this party, do you?"

Toni did mind. Very much. But Jana was already mumbling, "Of course not."

Toni had no choice but to move over and make room for him on her side of the table. She had perversely thought about just letting him stand there, but then decided that if that would make anyone look foolish, it would only be herself.

"You were saying that you got tied up?" Jana prompted, groping for some tidbit to latch on to.

"Traffic," Todd supplied, scanning Jana's menu. "It was worse than usual tonight, wasn't it, Kyle?"

"It's all the work they're doing on the streets." Kyle seemed impervious to the strain threading the conversation. He took off his tie and stuffed it into his jacket pocket, appearing quite unconcerned with the icy reception he was getting on his left. "Can I see your menu?"

Toni handed it to him. The feel of his fingers as they brushed against hers threatened to unravel the tenuous hold she had on her rapidly fraying nerves. There had been no need for him to touch her at all.

A taunting flicker of acknowledgment met his eyes as she quickly withdrew her hand. "Anything look good to you?"

You do, she sighed inwardly. "Not really."

She'd lost her appetite. And as soon as she could figure out how to do so gracefully, she'd leave. She should have left the second she'd seen him walk in. He wasn't being fair. Not to her. And certainly not to Jana and Todd by putting them in this awkward position. Kyle never had cared who got in his way when he was after something.

"Will you excuse me, please?" She managed a tight smile toward Kyle after she picked up her purse. She had to have a logical reason to make him move without arousing his suspicions, or causing a scene. There was only one thing she could think of that he couldn't argue with. "I have to go to the ladies' room."

The mistrust she expected lurked beneath the heavy slants of his dark eyebrows. But he did stand up—and offer her his hand.

Wanting to appear casual, she took it. She needed its support anyway.

The instant he released his grip—had he felt how badly she was shaking?—she headed straight for the door and out into the parking lot. Tomorrow she'd call Jana and find out how much she owed her for the drinks. Better yet, maybe Jana would stick Kyle with the bill.

"That was rude."

Toni didn't even break stride and continued to her car. She should have known that he would follow her. "Don't talk to me about being rude. What you just did was inexcusable."

"We were only going to have dinner with friends. What's so inexcusable about that?"

How could he be so insensitive? "Kyle, please . . . I don't want to argue with you."

She stopped next to her car, fumbling with her keys.

Kyle stood beside her, his hands jammed into his pockets. "I don't want to argue either, princess."

Since her eyes were fixed on the lock of the door, she couldn't see his expression. She didn't have to though. The deep resonance in his voice told her more than she wanted to know.

"Then, don't say another word," she begged, and watched her keys fall to the ground. She grabbed them before Kyle could, but he was now standing much too close.

"Come back inside with me. We'll have dinner, then go someplace where we can be alone to . . ."

She tilted her head back to meet the soft plea in his eyes. "You're expecting far too much, Kyle. There's no way you and I can have a nice, chatty little dinner with friends when there's so much unresolved between us. We can't ask Todd and Jana to . . ."

This time he interrupted. "You're admitting that there's something between us that's still unresolved?"

She glanced away. "Unfortunate choice of words," she said, defensively, and tried to put her key into the lock again. "I'm not admitting anything."

Kyle's hand folded over hers, his other one settling on her shoulder. "You haven't denied anything either."

His touch was gentle, undemanding. And his fingers slipped easily through her cold ones.

She wished she could feel something besides the strange sense of the inevitable that was sweeping through her. There was only one way she could keep him from torturing her like this. Only one thing she could say that would finally make him leave her alone so the wounds would begin to heal.

There was a deep sadness in her eyes when she slowly uncurled her fingers and lifted them to trace the chiseled line of his jaw.

One last time she would touch him. One last

time, she would feel that beautifully molded mouth against hers.

Raising her other hand, she pushed her fingers through the soft black hair at the back of his head and drew it toward her.

Kyle did nothing to discourage her. But he took no initiative either. His only response was to taste her lips as tenderly as she was tasting his, and to dig his fingers a little deeper into the jacket covering her shoulder.

She pulled away to meet the question smoldering in his eyes.

"You win," she conceded with a tremulous smile. "You said that all I had to do was tell you that I don't love you and you'd leave me alone." The keys in her hand bit into her palm, but that pain was nothing compared to the one twisting through her heart. She allowed herself one last look at his tightly held features, then turned away. "I don't love you, Kyle."

Chapter Nine

*K*yle didn't try to stop her when she slid inside her car. But just as she closed the door, he jerked it back open.

"You're a lot better at denying yourself what you want than I am, Toni."

She drew a trembling breath and tried to put the key into the ignition. "It's impossible to deny yourself something you can't have."

"Did it ever occur to you that one of the things you want is something I can't give you?" A moment ago frustration had tinted his tone. Now, he sounded angry. "That it might be something I want, too, but . . . Oh, forget it," he grated, adding an imprecation she couldn't quite hear.

She jumped when, a second later, he slammed the door—confusion joining hurt as she watched him disappear back through the parking lot.

Three minutes ago she had wanted nothing more than to put physical distance between them. Now, it was all she could do to keep from running after him. Would her heart and her head ever come to terms?

There wasn't a cloud in the sky on Saturday morning. It was one of those crisp fall days that invigorates the senses and heightens one's awareness to the change of seasons. The brisk, clean air reddened her cheeks and the faint smell of burning leaves made the rustle of those crunching beneath Toni's rhythmically pounding feet more noticeable somehow. It was a day to be shared. But the only person she wanted to share it with wasn't with her.

It was her own fault. If she had just left things alone, let their relationship remain the friendly, companionable one it had always been, none of this would have happened. She would still have Kyle to talk to.

As much as she missed being in Kyle's arms, she missed their sometimes bantering, other times serious, conversations more. She missed her best friend.

Leaving the jogging path, she cut across the play yard toward the duck pond. The squeals and laughter of the children tumbling down slides and begging their mothers to push them higher —"Higher, mommy!"—on the swings assailed her wind-numbed ears.

Children.

Years ago she had clung to an idealized fantasy of herself dressed in a frilly apron, tending to a nursery full of pink-cheeked babies while sending an imaginary husband off to work from a house in the suburbs. And over the years she had come to realize why she had conjured up that idyllic fantasy. She'd been an only child, one who'd spent most of her time in boarding schools, receiving little more than an occasional letter or gift from a mother who was never there. Her visions of domestic perfection had been nothing more than an escape from emotional loneliness.

Then she encountered the real world and a sense of practicality had taken over. The romantic lived on in her soul, but the dreams changed. She wasn't the frilly-apron type at all. The thought of spending all day cooped up with a houseful of children lost its appeal. She was a businesswoman, one with a much more realistic picture of the future. If she was ever blessed with a child, it would be because she and the man who shared her love needed to share it with another human being.

But the man she loved didn't love her. And as for a child . . .

She quickened her pace when she hit the path around the pond and tried to push the unwanted thoughts away. The track was filled with other joggers, and if any one of them paid any attention to the slender young woman in the lavender sweatsuit, they probably thought the tears she wiped from her eyes every fourth step were only caused by the cold.

Kyle was sitting on a bench in another park several miles away.

Wiping the dirt and perspiration from his face

with his towel, he watched the other men come off the field and head to their cars. He was glad the game was over. His mind just hadn't been on it today.

It was on the woman he loved, the woman he had given no choice but to say that she didn't love him.

He'd known all along how he'd felt about Toni. He just hadn't allowed himself to verbalize that emotion because it implied responsibilities he couldn't live up to. He still couldn't give her the security she wanted, but he owed them both a little honesty for a change.

"Hey, Donovan!" Todd broke away from the group in the parking lot and stopped in front of Kyle. "You want to come have a beer?"

Kyle absently rubbed his unshaven cheek. "Thanks. But I think I'll pass."

"No luck, huh?"

Kyle's gaze shifted from Todd's worn-out tennis shoes to his scruffy sweatshirt. Though Todd hadn't said anything about Tuesday night, Kyle knew what he was talking about. It had been Todd's idea to make a foursome out of dinner, and Kyle had thought it might be a good way to reestablish the companionship he and Toni had once shared. It had been an incredibly asinine thought.

"No," he conceded. "No luck."

Todd shrugged, his mouth twisting sympathetically, and walked off—leaving Kyle to contemplate the first step he needed to take. He had to talk to Toni—somewhere where there would be no interruptions and she didn't have any excuse to leave. The only place that met those requirements was her house. So the first thing he had to do was find out where she was living.

That meant going to see the man she had run to when she'd left him. If he remembered correctly, Toni had mentioned once that the Westline Clinic was open until two o'clock on Saturdays.

Kyle made it to the clinic by one, prepared to choke Toni's address out of the good doctor if he had to. He never had liked Greg Nichols.

Attitudes change. Drastically sometimes.

When Kyle walked out of the clinic over two hours later—totally amazed at how skillfully Greg had drawn him out—he felt dazed. He had just been handed a fighting chance at the ultimate reprieve. And, as far as he was concerned, Greg Nichols was the greatest guy on earth.

Kyle leaned against the fender of his car and stared down at the piece of paper Toni's address was written on. His hand was shaking so badly he couldn't even read it.

Toni had thought about going in to the office when she'd returned from the park. But that idea was quickly axed. It would only be a waste of time. She needed some kind of escape, but work wasn't it. What she needed was a vacation —to someplace warm like Hawaii, or the Sahara desert.

She was freezing. Though she'd been home for hours, the chill that had seeped into her bones while she'd been running felt like it was going to be permanent. Even her knees were cold. And the blasted furnace was out of whack. It was all of thirty-five degrees outside, and she could have sworn that it wasn't much more than that in her tiny house. She should have taken the condo Greg had offered. It had a fireplace. It didn't come with furniture though. If she had the choice now . . .

Tucking her jean-clad legs beneath her on the brown plaid loveseat, she pulled her blanket up to her shoulders and cast a longing glance at the wood coffee table. Greg would probably get upset with her if she made a fire with it. He probably wouldn't like what it would do to the carpet either.

If only Kyle were here to warm her.

"Stop it!" she admonished herself, and jerked her eyes back to the novel she'd been trying to read. The book was supposed to help her *not* think about him, but it was having just the opposite effect. She should have picked up a murder mystery instead of one of those addictive romances Madeline had gotten her hooked on. Reading about two people making love in a snowed-in mountain cabin was only conjuring up visions of the man she didn't want to think about. Besides, the setting wasn't exactly taking her mind off of how cold she was. All that icy wind and blowing snow and . . .

The loud ring of the telephone on the end table next to her turned her shiver into a start. She grabbed for the receiver before it could ring again.

"You must have been sitting on it." She heard Greg chuckle—and that put an end to the anticipation she told herself she hadn't felt in the first place. It wouldn't have been Kyle anyway. As far as she knew, he didn't have her number.

"Just about," she smiled. "Are you calling as my client, my landlord"—there was no need to mention the broken furnace to him. She'd already called his property manager who'd said it would be fixed . . . sometime Monday—"or as a 'friendly' doctor?"

"A bit of the latter. Is Kyle there?"

She felt her heart skip a beat, then resume its pace in her throat. "Kyle? Why would he be here?"

"That must mean that he isn't yet," Greg observed quickly. "Just give him a message for me when he gets there. Tell him that I checked those dates. We had talked about either the fifteenth or the seventeenth, but the twenty-first is all that's available if he still wants to do it. Or maybe I should say, if he still has a reason to." There was a suggestion of a smile in his voice. "Anyway, I'll be out of town the first part of next week and he said he wouldn't be available the following Thursday or Friday, but I will need to see him at least a week before. Got that?"

She most definitely did not! Kyle was on his way here? Greg and Kyle had talked to each other? About what?

She hardly knew which question to ask first. "Greg, I . . . just a minute."

A car door had just slammed outside. Dropping the receiver, she whipped back the blanket and scrambled to her feet.

Kyle's head snapped up the second she opened the door. His expression held the most discordant mix of elation and anxiety she had ever seen. Her own revealed nothing but confusion.

"Greg wants to talk to you." She crossed her

arms to grip the sleeves of her bulky turquoise sweater and watched his eyebrows scrunch together. "He's on the phone."

"Did he say anything to you?"

"Nothing that made any sense."

She didn't know if it was relief or disquiet that met his cool gray eyes. He just gave her a tight nod and moved past her when she stepped back to let him in.

"Over there." She pointed to the telephone, then closed the door to lean against it.

Kyle snatched up the receiver. "Yeah, Greg?"

Toni dug her sock-covered toes into the tan carpet and wished her heart would stop beating in her ears so she could hear. A minute ago, it had been thudding in her throat. What was it about the mere mention of Kyle, let alone his presence, that caused her heart to forget its proper place? Maybe she had some physical abnormality she should talk to Greg about.

Kyle wasn't saying much anyway. Nothing other than an occasional "Uh-huh" or "Right" while he paced between the loveseat and the coffee table. The phone cord was too short for him to go anywhere else.

Her confusion over what was going on didn't allow her to focus on the problem that still existed between her and Kyle. Her normally analytical, practical mind was much too muddled to deal with logic.

And it was very illogical to be standing there sinking her nails into her arms and admiring the snug fit of his jeans and the way his charcoal turtleneck sweater so perfectly molded his long back and broad shoulders. The motion of his hand as he drew it through his black hair brought her attention to the wealth of silver threading it. Even dressed as he was, as alternately agitated and controlled as she seemed, he still managed to exude a brand of distinguished masculinity that few men could ever hope to perfect.

What woman in her right mind would give him up? some devilish voice inquired from within. An equally illusive voice responded. *A woman who is nothing without the courage of her convictions.* The first voice responded. *Fool!*

"That all depends on her," Kyle was saying, and Toni quashed both mental advocates as she jerked her eyes to his face. He was watching her guardedly. "Don't worry," he assured Greg, turning away again, "I'll let you know, and I don't think your calling here hurt anything. I would have been here sooner, but I needed some time to reevaluate my position, so to speak."

Whatever Greg's response was must have been amusing. Kyle chuckled quietly. Then, mumbling his thanks, he hung up.

For a moment, he just stood there with his back to her and his hand resting on the phone. For that same moment, Toni thought about retrieving her blanket from the loveseat and wrapping it around her shivering body—even as a hundred questions skittered through her mind. She didn't know if she wanted to get that close to him, or which question he'd be most likely to answer.

"My God," he muttered, eyeing the blanket

and then the way she was running her hands over her arms. "Didn't he rent you any heat with this place?"

"The furnace is broken."

"Do you have any brandy?"

"Are you *that* cold?"

"I'm not. But you are. You're shaking like a leaf."

She was. And as much as she hated to admit it, it was more from nerves than anything else. When was he going to get to the point? Whatever it was.

The brandy suddenly sounded like a good idea. "It's in the kitchen."

"Then let's go get you some. I could use it myself."

A minute later, she understood why.

Kyle stayed in the doorway of the compact kitchen while she filled her only coffee cup with Grand Marnier. When she handed it to him, she couldn't help but notice the tremor in his hand.

"We'll have to share it," she said, trying to imagine what could affect someone as strong as Kyle like that. She turned to put the bottle away. "I don't have any glasses." All of her things were in transit from New York.

"I love you, Toni."

If the bottom of the bottle hadn't just hit the shelf, it would have been a hundred brown fragments on the floor. As it was, her numb fingers fell limply to her side and she turned to lean against the counter. "What did you say?"

Kyle had put the cup down, and two strides placed him in front of her. She saw his chest expand with his deeply drawn breath and felt its quiet expulsion on the top of her head. It was almost as if he were trying to gather the courage to repeat the words she couldn't believe she'd just heard.

"I said, I love you." He spoke more quietly this time, and the touch of his fingers on her cheek was tentative and light.

Bewildered, afraid to acknowledge the voice that was telling her everything would be all right for fear that the hurt would only be compounded when she discovered that it wasn't, she could only stare up into those velvety gray eyes. The love she couldn't deny found its counterpart there, and the unwanted intrusion of reason was forgotten.

For once, her heart was beating in its proper place. "I love you, too, Kyle," she whispered, touching the hard line of his jaw as timorously as he was her more delicate one. "I always have."

He took her cold fingers from his cheek and brought them to his lips. His mouth felt firm and warm against the pads of her fingers. Warmer still when he pressed them to her forehead.

An instant later, she was in his arms. A fevered sense of desperation telegraphed itself from one to the other. For now, this was all they needed. To allow themselves the simple security of just being held by the person they loved.

"Oh, princess," he finally breathed. "There's so much I have to say to you."

The heat of his body had brought a reactive shudder. Another darted through her when he moved back, withholding the kiss she now wanted so badly. He must have wanted it, too.

His eyes had fallen to her mouth, and she could see his need wrestling with control.

Control won. "Come on." He slipped his arm back around her shoulder and picked up the cup from the counter. "We need to talk."

The seriousness in his tone, and the way he gulped down a swallow of the brandy, abruptly shadowed Toni's euphoria. Tucking her legs back under the blanket, she took a healthy sip herself.

"I suppose you're wondering what that conversation with Greg was all about." He sat down several inches away and leaned forward to clasp his hands between his knees. Her response was unnecessary, and he continued without waiting for one. "I went to see him to get your address and"—he made a sound that was somewhere between a disbelieving sigh and an incredulous laugh—"and walked out with that, and him as my doctor."

Toni's eyebrows shot together. "Your doctor? He's a gynecologist!" She took another swallow of brandy, a bigger one this time. Why would a man go to a gynecologist?

Kyle must have thought her expression amusing. His lips tightened as if he were trying to suppress a smile, but in the next instant his jaw had tensed. "He's also a reproductive endocrinologist," he supplied quietly.

Toni knew that. "So?"

"Which is medical jargon for . . . ?"

She shrugged. Apparently he wanted her to fill in the blank. "Infertility specialist," she responded—and met Kyle's steady, knowing gaze.

Every nerve in her body went numb.

Infertility. Children. He had said he didn't want them. Had he meant that he couldn't *have* them?

A wave of understanding washed over her before he even began to speak.

"That's why Lynn left me." His gaze returned to his hands. "She said there was no point in staying with someone who was only half a man."

It had cost him a lot to say that, and he didn't have to explain the devastation that that unfeeling label must have wreaked on a man with as much pride as he had.

"After a while," he continued, "I managed to convince myself that kids weren't important . . . that I never really wanted a family anyway. I had my work and . . ."

As he spoke, Toni was beginning to see how he had turned inward his desire for something he thought he could never have. How he had forced himself to make up for his "inadequacy" by determining to be the best at everything else. It didn't take a degree in psychology to see that the compulsion that had driven him so long ago— the need to get the accounts, the deals, even the women he wanted—had only been a need to prove to himself that he was as much of a man as the next guy.

"I guess what it boiled down to"—he was gripping his hands so hard that his knuckles were white—"was that I was so afraid of having whatever you felt for me turn into the same bitterness Lynn felt, that I just couldn't face the fact that it was something you had every right to know. When I said I didn't see any point in our getting married, all I was doing was avoiding the issue . . . and you meant too much to me to let you walk away without thinking that I don't love you."

He took a deep breath, and when he turned his head toward her she could see a strange excitement flickering in his eyes. It was there in his voice, too. "Before I went to see Greg, that was all I was going to say, but now . . . I do want to marry you, Toni. And maybe I have a chance to give you what you want. He told me about this new procedure. . . ."

Toni was feeling a lot of things. An almost uncontainable happiness. Sympathy. Affection. Love. And woven through it all, exasperation.

Kyle was not a man who responded to sympathy. That would be the last thing he'd want. Knowing that whatever she said would have to be put delicately though, she set the cup of brandy next to the phone and searched for the proper words.

"For cripe sake, Donovan," she muttered, leaning across him to grab his hands and make him face her. She'd been aching to touch him. "Stop talking like you're some steer that isn't marketable unless you can produce a calf!" So much for delicate. They'd always communicated better when they didn't mince words anyway. "I love *you*, not your reproductive capabilities." She wanted to hear what else he had to say, but first she wanted him to know for certain that *he* mattered more than anything else.

Her last remark was loaded with possibilities.

And when she saw that wonderful, teasing smile lightening his features, she knew she was in for it.

He shook his head slowly. "You could have fooled me." His dark eyes caressed her from the top of her head to her knees, and back up again. "I was under the impression that there were certain aspects of those capabilities that you . . ."

"Be serious!"

His smile deepened. "I am."

"You're getting off the subject," she reminded him, not wanting to move from where she was pressed against his side. She wanted him to get back to this marriage thing, then tell her what Greg had said.

Kyle shifted toward her, his motion making her release his hands. Taking her by the arms, he pushed her down onto the cushions, settling his weight on his elbows and covering her body with his. "I thought it was very much a part of the subject," he returned. He propped his chin in his hand and pushed the hair back from her forehead with the other. He could feel her small breasts crushed to his chest and the friction of her hips as she shifted beneath him. Suddenly, it was a little difficult to remember what else needed to be said. "Maybe we should . . ."

Toni's finger stilled his words.

"You told me the other night that I was better at denying myself what I want than you are." Her voice was soft, filled with wonder at how instantly her body had responded to the feel of his. "But you were wrong. I want to kiss you, and I don't want to deny myself a minute longer."

"Oh, Toni." The tight groan of longing rumbled in his chest, and his lips met hers.

The tenderness of their kiss, the way his mouth barely touched hers when her tongue traced a tantalizing path along the firm line of his bottom lip, then dipped inward to tangle with the touch of his own, quickly turned to a hunger that threatened to consume them both.

She clung to him, feeling the lean muscles in his back tensing as he molded her hips into more intimate alignment, delighting in the solid feel of his body and pulling his weight fully upon her. There were still words that needed to be said, matters to be discussed. But what they were communicating to each other now was just as important.

His hands were working under her sweater, their warmth melting the pervading chill that had been shuddering through her only moments before. The tremors coursing through her now had nothing to do with the cold. And the answering tremble rippling his length spoke in answering need. She felt her arms being pulled from her sleeves and he lifted his head only long enough to pull the soft wool over hers and toss it and her scant pink bra to the floor. Then he was pressing her back down and murmuring her name over and over as he rained tormenting kisses from her ear to her throat and down to capture the turgid bud of her breast. Toni gasped at the shock of pleasure his tongue, his lips, his teeth, elicited. His caress was so loving, and so gentle.

She drew her fingertips through the crispness of his hair, moving them slowly over the back of his head to dip below the collar of his sweater. His flesh was warm and hard—and that small contact wasn't enough.

A tiny whimper caught in her throat when he slid his hand behind her back and moved to her other breast. His touch was like velvet fire, her own an impatient plea to rid him of the fabric that kept the feel of his skin from her. Kyle understood the urgent motions of her hands. They had followed the line of his back downward toward his belt.

Seconds later, his sweater joined hers. The hair on his chest tantalized her sensitive breasts. The motion of his hand as he pushed the weight of one upward when he fastened his lips over hers once more brought a stab of exquisite heat to shimmer inward, then down.

"I love you, princess," he rasped, tumbling them both to the floor and pulling the blanket over them. "I want to make love with you knowing what it's like to say and really mean those words." He moved his hand between them and caught the snap of her jeans. "And to have you mean them."

Over and over she whispered those words. The confining garments were gone. There was nothing to separate the silkiness of her skin from the coarse smoothness of his. His hands drifted over her body. His sensual, provocative words urging her with their erotic poetry. Everywhere his tongue touched her, she burned. And she knew her own caresses, the subtle and seductive motions he had taught her, were provoking that same honeyed heat in him.

"Please, Kyle," she pleaded, needing the release only he could give her—wanting the fervid tension to last forever. "Please. I need you."

She arched against him, feeling his rigidity pressing against her. And then he was pulling back, poised above her.

"Look at me." His voice was thick and laced with desire.

Her lids felt heavy. But she met the intensity in his eyes and saw the passion tightening his features as he tucked his hand beneath her hips and slowly entered her waiting warmth.

It was the tenderest of possessions. And then the fiercest. A culmination filled with so much need and love that the physical explosion of release that followed was only the final melding of two souls already irrevocably fused. And when the world righted itself long minutes later, the universe had expanded to accommodate the larger oneness they had created.

The blanket lay in a tangled heap beside them, and Toni curled against the warmth of Kyle's chest. His leg was draped over hers, his fingers wending lazily over her arm.

"Your skin feels like satin," he whispered, nuzzling her temple with his lips. "And sandpaper."

A quizzical little laugh threaded her husky voice. "Sandpaper?" That wasn't very romantic!

"Mmmm," he mumbled, groping above his head for something. "All those goosebumps."

She hadn't even noticed. But now that he had mentioned it . . . "What are you"—he had put his hand on top of her head to get better leverage, and she felt the scratch of her sweater

brush her neck when he pulled her upright—
"doing?"

Her last word was muffled by the turquoise
wool being jerked over her head.

"Dressing you. The last thing I want is for you
to catch pneumonia. And there's still a couple of
things we need to talk about." Her head popped
out of the tight collar, and she met his wide grin.
"We did get a little sidetracked, you know."

"I guess we did." Was the smile on her face as
silly as she thought it was?

That smile relaxed as she reached for Kyle's
sweater and she traded him that for her socks. It
was probably better to concentrate on getting
dressed rather than allow herself the distracting
pleasure of watching him dress himself—so she
turned and stood up to pull on her jeans. Though
she had been thoroughly satisfied by their lovemaking, her need for him seemed insatiable.
The sight of his naked perfection did nothing to
alleviate that need.

Clothed now, she ran her fingers through her
tousled hair and glanced over to see Kyle frowning at her while he tucked his sweater into his
waistband.

She matched her expression to his and picked
up the blanket. "What's the matter?"

"Why'd you cut it?"

Her hand flew back to her hair. Then, she
shrugged. "For a couple of reasons." She resumed her former place on the loveseat. "It was
a hassle to take care of . . . and every time I took
it down, it reminded me of someone I was trying
to forget."

The muscle in his jaw bunched, which didn't agree at all with the smile he was trying to manage. He said nothing else about it though. Apparently, her honest answer had left no room for comment.

His odd mix of reactions brought a reminder of what she had been thinking about while lying peacefully in his arms. She understood now why Kyle had been so driven when she first met him. What she didn't understand was what had happened during those intervening years that had tempered that outward aggression. So she asked him—and that question brought his familiar grin when he sat down beside her.

"I once knew this very opinionated, rather irritating young woman who had the audacity to tell me . . . her boss . . . that if I didn't get rid of the chip on my shoulder, I'd probably run myself right into an early grave, and that she'd be the only friend I had who'd attend my funeral." He reached for her hand and curved his fingers through hers. "If I remember right, I think I told her where she could go with her advice."

That was the day Toni had fallen in love with him the first time. He'd told her where to go all right, but he'd done it with that beautifully sexy grin of his that had left her almost paralyzed.

"It took a long time for that advice to sink in. . . ." His eyes caressed her face as he brought her fingers to his lips. ". . . And even longer for me to admit to you why that chip was there."

She smiled softly and squeezed his hand. He'd had no reason to tell her then, and they both knew it.

Kyle's expression sobered. "This procedure Greg told me about . . ."

The time for less significant questions was over. Kyle wanted to deal in realities now, and Toni quietly accepted what he presented as the cold, hard facts. She hated the thought of him having to undergo surgery. It was obvious enough that he was nervous about it, but at the same time she had never seen him so absorbed or excited about anything. The only thing that saved his graphic description of both the male anatomy and how the correction was supposed to work from being embarrassing was his fascination with the whole process. He talked about it like Greg was an auto mechanic who was going to fix a broken fuel pump.

When Kyle had finished his explanation, he uncoiled their hands and drew his finger down her cheek. "So how about it, princess?" he asked quietly. "Will you marry me and take the risk? He said there's only a fifty-fifty chance that it will work, but . . ."

Toni placed a quieting finger on his mouth, her eyes filled with the love that had its beginnings five long years ago. "We take worse risks than that every day in the stockmarket." Kyle had taught her how to take those chances. "And even if we never have children, we'll always have each other."

He swallowed convulsively and cupped her face between his hands. "You know something?" His thumb trailed over her bottom lip. "I think I'm going to like spending forever with my best friend."

Epilogue

The assistant Toni had hired four years earlier worked out remarkably well. Toni no longer worked on weekends and, as far as she was concerned, they were now the best part of the week. Kyle didn't play football anymore though. The game had fizzled out after Todd moved to California and a few of the other regulars had lost interest. Kyle had found other ways to occupy himself on Saturdays.

"Is Kyle still downstairs?" she asked Madeline, who was bustling down the hall with an armload of laundry. The woman who had become one part housekeeper and nine parts family lived with them now.

"Still in the weight room. Never have understood his preoccupation with those machines." Her gray curls bounced as she shook her head and walked off humming to herself.